SO-BFF-608

"You've Got to Let Me Explain, Erica."

"How can you explain?" she demanded. "You think that no one can love me for myself, only for my money." She was furious—and deeply hurt.

"Don't be ridiculous," he said in a savage tone. "Do you think what happened in Miami was because of money?"

"Yes. It was all part of your plan. It's some kind of joke with you—trying to take over my company and making love to me on the side."

"Never mind, Erica," he said angrily. "I won't be bothering you again."

PAT WALLACE
lives in New York's Greenwich Village with her husband, who is the inspiration for all her heroes. She is also devoted to their several cats and to her writing, at which she has been very successful for many years.

Dear Reader,

Silhouette Special Editions are an exciting new line of contemporary romances from Silhouette Books. Special Editions are written specifically for our readers who want a story with heightened romantic tension.

Special Editions have all the elements you've enjoyed in Silhouette Romances and *more*. These stories concentrate on romance in a longer, more realistic and sophisticated way, and they feature greater sensual detail.

I hope you enjoy this book and all the wonderful romances from Silhouette. We welcome any suggestions or comments and invite you to write to us at the address below.

Karen Solem
Editor-in-Chief
Silhouette Books
P.O. Box 769
New York, N. Y. 10019

PAT WALLACE
Silver Fire

Silhouette Special Edition
Published by Silhouette Books New York
America's Publisher of Contemporary Romance

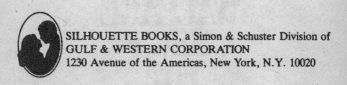

SILHOUETTE BOOKS, a Simon & Schuster Division of
GULF & WESTERN CORPORATION
1230 Avenue of the Americas, New York, N.Y. 10020

Copyright © 1982 by Pat Wallace

Distributed by Pocket Books

All rights reserved, including the right to reproduce
this book or portions thereof in any form whatsoever.
For information address Silhouette Books, 1230
Avenué of the Americas, New York, N.Y. 10020

ISBN: 0-671-53556-0

First Silhouette Books printing November, 1982

10 9 8 7 6 5 4 3 2 1

All of the characters in this book are fictitious. Any resemblance to actual persons, living or dead, is purely coincidental.

Map by Ray Lundgren

SILHOUETTE, SILHOUETTE SPECIAL EDITION
and colophon are trademarks of Simon & Schuster.

America's Publisher of Contemporary Romance

Printed in the U.S.A.

For
Ola English,
Willeen Bennett, and
Neil Robinson Wallace

Many thanks to my dear friend
Fran Glasgow
for help with San Francisco

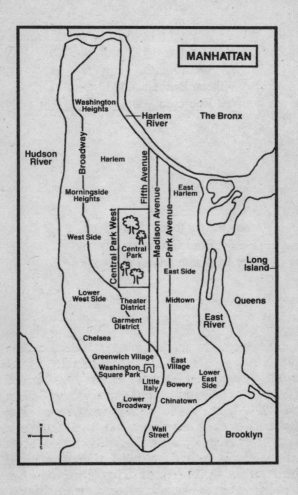

Chapter One

"There they blow." Erica Warren, sighting the ships' masts along Manhattan's South Street Seaport, grinned at Morgan Hunt. She braked her Mercedes in front of the oyster bar on Fulton Street. The car was a rich dark brown that matched her eyes, a perfect foil for its driver's beauty. Her hair, done in the smooth new style of the coming season, glowed with the vivid auburn of an October leaf. This afternoon her velvet-brown eyes were sheltered from the autumn sun by big umber-shaded glasses; they gave her small face a pixie look.

"You passed Sweets," Morgan said in his carefully casual way.

"I feel like the oyster bar, if you don't mind. It's more . . . anonymous." She knew she was being contrary, but after a day like today she needed to escape. It had been the kind of day Morgan thrived on—a busy, embattled morning on "the Street." He'd suggested the cocktail lounge at Windows on the World, atop the World Trade Center, but Erica had had a sudden yearning for the water.

"I adore you," he said, "but I'll never understand you. Why that scruffy little place? They know us at Sweets and we can get proper service."

"That's just it; I don't feel 'proper.' And at Sweets I'm the 'Baby Tycoon.' "

The press had saddled her with that name; at twenty-two, Erica had inherited Warren Industries, the transportation empire of her lovable grandfather, eccentric Josh Warren. When Erica, an only child, had lost both her parents in a plane crash six years before, old Josh had started grooming the eighteen-year-old girl as his heir. He had come to believe that when he was gone she'd be the logical one to take over the business. His conservative attorneys tried to reason with him, without success. "What about your grandsons?" the scandalized advisers demanded.

"What about them?" the crusty Josh returned. "Jack was the only one worth a nickel and he died in Vietnam. Roger thinks he's John Barrymore; unfortunately he's not. All he cares about are reviews and dividends. He thinks the fairies bring profits during the night. As for George . . . well, let him ruin his father's business. He won't ruin mine. Erica's worth more than the lot of them." The advisers protested that she was far too young.

"If women are going to have any sense at all," Josh countered, "they have more at twenty-one than most men do at thirty. Women don't run after topless dancers or lose a fortune in Vegas. Watch 'em; they're the ones who put coins in the one-arm bandits. Erica knows how to count a penny; I taught her myself."

Josh Warren had died two years ago at the ripe age of eighty-four; on Erica's twenty-second birthday she acquired forty-nine percent of the stock in Warren Industries. The irascible Josh commented in his will that Erica was not being given fifty-two percent; she'd have to fight for control, as he had. Otherwise there wouldn't be "any fun in it at all." By then she had already had years of training for her new role.

Adoring her grandfather, Erica had emulated him in everything. She could sail a boat by the time she was thirteen; at seventeen she was familiar with the language of stock manipulation. She bought and sold her own shares, making herself a tidy profit. While her schoolmates were squealing at rock groups and deciding whom they would marry, Erica was studying company prospectuses and learning foreign languages. The approving Josh told her she had a genius for finance.

The old man saw much of his own drive and

daring in the fragile, auburn-haired girl. "You'll do me proud," he told her a few months before he died. "There's one thing, though, my dear . . . don't forget you're a woman. More than anything else I wish you happiness in love, the kind of happiness I had with your grandmother."

Erica thought about that now, sitting in the Mercedes on this bright early-autumn afternoon beside Morgan Hunt. She had been achingly lonely in the years since Josh's death. He'd been everything to her—father, mother, teacher, best friend. She needed to be close to someone again, but she wasn't sure that someone was Morgan. She was often sharp and contrary with him, but there was something in his bland correctness that brought out the devil in her. She wondered if Josh had ever approved of him—their families were neighbors—but she didn't think so. She gave Morgan a quick side glance.

He was wearing his customary "Wall Street chic" garb: a wide, sober tie; a discreet version of the semi-western suits that looked so wrong on most urban men; well-shined boots. He had just the right amount of blond hair. He never surprised her in any way at all.

With Morgan there had never been that "silver fire in the blood," a phrase she'd seen in an old book of poems and never forgotten. It was a feeling she had only dreamed of having. She'd been too cautious—too busy, for one thing—to do the things her friends had hinted at. No one ever lit that "silver fire" in her veins and she wondered if there was anyone who could.

"You're very thoughtful," Morgan said. "Aren't you hungry at all?"

"Not very." She knew what Morgan was going to say.

He said it. "You've got to eat. You said you didn't have breakfast and here it is almost three o'clock." She glanced at the gold watch on her left wrist. Good heavens, it *was* late.

"You need to eat more," he went on. "You look as if a stiff breeze would blow you away." She silently admitted the truth of that. When she had gotten dressed that morning, lightly making up her face, she had noticed that her cheekbones were more prominent than they had been, her body fragile in the plaid shirt dress of crepe de chine. Her bracelet felt heavy on her right wrist. But the dress did a lot for her slimness; instead of a collar, it had a scarf attached to its deeply veed neckline. Its colors—dark brown and turquoise on cream—pointed up her touch of golden tan and harmonized with the small loop earrings studded with Australian opals.

"You've got to keep up your strength," Morgan added, "if you're going to wage a war with the board . . . and George."

Erica heard the oblique reproach in his comment. He always accused her of "making waves" on Wall Street and usually sided with her cousin George, who headed his late father's ad agency but was also a member of Warren's board.

"Please! I'd like to forget the office for a while. I'll make a deal with you: I'll go to Sweets if we can look at the ships first. Okay?"

"Okay." Morgan sounded resigned. "You're an apple off the old tree, darling. You sound just like your grandfather." He smiled to take any sting from his comment. "But not a long look, please. I'm starving. I could eat this steering wheel."

She had to laugh. "Fair enough. I just want a breath of wind." She realized that her grandfather had always said that, instead of a breath of air. Erica picked up her taupe envelope bag from the seat, dropped her car keys in it and opened the door for herself. She never waited for Morgan to get out and open it for her. He was used to that and other signs of her "liberation" and no longer protested. Perversely, Erica wished he would. To make up for her own contrariness she took Morgan's arm and smiled up at him. He softened at once.

Morgan was really an attractive man; she couldn't understand why he left her so cold. Maybe part of it was his closeness to George. She and George had never gotten along. Morgan was slender, clean-cut, tall, with finely chiseled features and healthy blond hair in contrast to skin kept tan all year under the sun lamps of his athletic club. His blue eyes were lively and amiable. He was quite . . . "presentable."

She examined the word. It was stuffy, like Morgan and his crowd. Who did she want to present him to, if it came to that? It was she who needed to be pleased.

But she stifled the thought and they strolled the few remaining yards down Fulton Street to the piers. Erica started walking to the left, barely glancing at the stolid training ship always anchored at the foot of Fulton. Her attention was caught by a strange sailing ship riding at anchor farther down the slip, beyond the familiar working boats the Seaport had preserved. People sometimes rented the small boats for receptions and cocktail parties. The sailing ship was no tame for-rent vessel; she was a clipper, magnificently restored, flying a brilliant crimson and bright-green flag.

"Why, she's a Portugee," Erica exclaimed, using Josh's nautical word for "Portuguese." Josh Warren had been a sailor when he was young and had been all over the world. He had always been a little contemptuous of the Hunts, who had a place on Long Island near the Warrens'. The Hunts had a motor yacht; Josh and Erica were challenged by the thrill of sails.

Erica took off her shadowy glasses; she felt as excited as a little girl. The sun had faded to a high cloudiness, and the afternoon wind, as it sometimes did in New York's exciting, changeable autumns, brought an edge of chill. Erica shivered. They were standing in the shade of the overpass, and the wind was sharp, but she was excited, not cold.

Morgan asked her something but she hardly heard. She felt utterly alone; the rising wind blew back her vivid hair and she raised her face to its caress.

"You look like that figurehead."

She started and asked, "What?" as if she had been awakened from a dream.

"I said, you look like the mermaid on that ship

with your hair blowing back that way." For the first time Erica noticed the carven mermaid on the clipper's prow; she had long, streaming hair and her face was delicate, elusive.

"But you must be cold," Morgan said.

"Cold!" Erica laughed. She had a hearty, free, unfeminine laugh that contradicted her looks, and it jarred the conservative Morgan. "Not a bit," she said. "You know I'm used to the water."

"That's true. I never heard you complain, even on the Island. For such a little thing you've got fantastic vigor. I think you live on air, Erica."

He had said that before and she hardly listened. She murmured, "It's wonderful here at night. Even when it rained that very cool night last month I didn't—" She stopped, feeling herself blush. She'd really put her foot in it now.

"What were you doing here that night? You told me you were too tired to go to the ballet."

Chagrined, she answered, "It was a sea-chantey concert."

She could feel his resentment, although he said nothing more. Many times when he'd asked her to go to the opera or ballet, to the theater or one of the less hectic discos, she'd put him off with feigned plans or fatigue. He was getting that stubborn look again; it probably meant he was going to propose tonight, something he'd done more than once.

"Had enough ships?" he asked, his voice a bit cool.

"Not quite." He seemed really irritated now,

but so was she, and she wished he'd just leave her there alone and go away.

"Well, watch your step," he said sullenly. "Don't catch your heels."

"Yes, Daddy," she mocked him, and she wasn't sure whether he was going to kiss her or spank her. He was only eight years older, yet he acted like a man of fifty sometimes. She knew he was too conservative to cope with the Josh streak in her. Erica thought, amused: My grandfather was hell on wheels. If only she could meet another man like him—but there probably weren't any, anymore.

Erica slipped out of Morgan's grasp and moved nearer to the edge of the pier. "Don't get too close," he warned. It was too late.

One of her delicate heels caught in an opening between the slats of the pier; she wriggled her foot and, leaning forward a little to disengage the heel, lost her balance and fell headlong into the water.

Morgan kicked off his shoes, about to dive in. Erica was a strong swimmer, but not in those clinging clothes, in that oily water. An enormous splash drenched Morgan, almost knocking him backward in his surprise.

Nettled, he saw a black-haired man with powerful shoulders and muscled arms swimming toward Erica, who was spluttering, treading water. Morgan was exasperated even more; she was laughing. Grimly the powerful swimmer reached the sodden Erica and she felt him grab her under the arms, his big hands carelessly cupping her breasts.

"What the devil are you laughing at?" the man shouted at her. "This water's filthy, you little fool!"

Morgan bellowed, "Don't you talk to her like that!"

The swimmer, easily treading water, turned his weathered face toward Morgan Hunt. His skin and hair were so dark that his light-gray eyes were startling in contrast; he was tanned almost to a mahogany shade.

"Well, keep her dry," he yelled. He was breathing fast from exertion and Erica could feel his chest against her side; it was very exciting.

"Bring her out, damn it." Morgan must be furious, she thought. He was always so careful of his speech around her. She felt another wave of laughter just about to break.

Her rescuer hauled her without ceremony onto the edge of the pier; his grasp was steely around her hips, pushing her up until she could reach a handhold. She grabbed the rough edge of the dock and clambered upward; her hands hurt. She saw with dismay that her skirt had risen high on her thighs. Things didn't seem so funny now.

As she scrambled over the side of the pier and stood up she looked down. The soaking dress clearly revealed the fullness of her breasts through the fragile bra and her long legs in their torn pantyhose were exposed almost to the waist. She struggled to pull the clinging fabric down over her body.

Morgan looked tactfully away. The dark man pulled himself up with the ease of an acrobat and stood staring at Erica, from her draggled hair to her feet, one foot in a stocking, the other still in a shoe. Annoyed, she kicked off the remaining shoe and saw the man's pale, fiery stare focus on her legs.

Blast him. She'd show him. As calmly as if they were being introduced at a party, she held out her hand, saying, "Thank you very much, Mr. ———?"

The man, who towered several inches over Morgan's six feet, smiled down at her, amused and admiring. "Nothing to it," he said curtly. "I'm always falling for women."

"Look here." Morgan's voice was sharp, but the man ignored him. "Just see here, fellow," Morgan said. This time the dark man looked at Morgan with an arrogant expression. He had thick, carelessly cut black hair; his broad chest was exposed and his huge forearms were bare. He looks like a pirate, Erica reflected, and just about as trustworthy. His pale eyes gleamed like silver in his deeply tanned face. And yet, for all his rough looks, his features and the shape of his head were proud and fine.

Erica was shaking with cold. Morgan took off his damp jacket and draped it carefully around her shoulders. She nodded her thanks but could not look away from the raffish stranger.

"You're from the . . ." She looked at the clipper for the name under the figurehead. *"Sereia de Madeira.* Thanks for saving me," she concluded flippantly. She smiled into the man's silvery eyes.

He had the grace to look chagrined. It seemed

to her that when she spoke the ship's name, "Siren of Madeira," he looked at her with more interest.

"Yes. I'm the . . . first mate of the *Sereia*." He repeated the name with a loving intonation, a singing sound. Erica, who knew some Portuguese, was thrilled by the way he spoke of the ship, as if he loved the sea the way she did herself. He was a very mysterious person. There was something challenging in his eyes—eyes that first mocked her as an empty-headed woman, then admired and provoked her at the same time. But now he was looking at her as if she were an unruly child and his expression irked her.

Morgan reached for the wallet in the inside pocket of his jacket. "Excuse me, Erica." He moved gingerly and took the wallet out without touching her breast, to which the wet fabric still clung provocatively. She saw a bright gleam in the stranger's eyes and was puzzled as to its meaning. Morgan took out a bill of large denomination and offered it to the sailor.

The dark man laughed out loud and then said politely, for him, "No, thanks, pal. It was a pleasure." Again the piercing eyes, like molten silver, examined Erica's face and body. "A pleasure I'd like to repeat . . . in cleaner water." He gave Erica another insolent look and without glancing again at Morgan turned on his heel and strode away. He walked as if he owned the city, thought Erica. She watched him board the clipper.

She turned to Morgan and said lightly, "Well, I

guess that takes care of Sweets. Or lunch, for that matter. I'm too messy even for the oyster bar. I smell like the Fulton Fish Market."

"You'd better let me take you home." Morgan grabbed her elbow and steered her toward South Street. "Speaking of fish, there's something fishy about that roughneck. I could swear I've seen him on the Street. Just can't figure it."

He'd looked familiar to Erica, too. She thought she'd seen a picture of him somewhere, but couldn't imagine in what context. She made no answer as they walked back toward the car.

"Don't bother with me, Morgan. Get some lunch." She opened the door and got in, thankful she still had her purse. It had dropped on the pier before she went in the drink. She took out her keys.

"Are you sure?" Morgan leaned into the open window. "I didn't like that fellow's looks. What if he . . . followed you?"

"That's unlikely." She was amazed that she felt almost regretful. "I'm sure I'm not his type."

Erica saw Morgan glance furtively at the top of her wet dress. "I don't like the way he looked at your . . . jewelry."

"My *jewelry!* How unflattering." Immediately she was sorry for the suggestive retort. Morgan was hard enough to handle now and she certainly didn't want to tease him.

He shook his head.

"Bye, bye," she said lightly and started the car.

"Erica, wait a minute."

She slowed down. She caught a glimpse of

herself in the driving mirror. Her hair was a wreck, but the wild ringlets made her look approachable and helpless and her eyes were big and bright. She assumed a cool expression as he asked, "What about tonight . . . is the play still on?"

"Oh, the play." She tried to keep her supreme disinterest from her voice. But seeing his eager face she relented and said, "Yes. All right."

"Dinner, too?" She nodded. "I've found a very special place," he added.

"Pick me up at six-thirty." He was like an insistent puppy.

He ignored her tone. "Dress up, darling. It's going to be a very special night."

That was it, then. He was going to propose again. The thought depressed her, but she managed a smile and drove away with a careless wave.

In the mirror she saw Morgan brush at his clothes, then walk toward Sweets. She wondered what it would be like to go there with the arrogant seaman.

As the Mercedes sped up the FDR Drive Erica felt a strange exhilaration. Her tumble had completely ruined her pretty new dress, worn for the first time that morning. And the incident had destroyed far more—her hard-gained self-confidence. She'd looked like a fool before that man. She had always tried hard to look older than she was, to hold her own with the board. And she was not easily embarrassed. Even as an adolescent her poise had been held up as an example to

her friends, lauded by their parents. Now for the
first time in years she felt awkward, frivolous
and young. Despite the constant battles with the
tough-minded board she had succeeded in
everything she tried, bringing a new energy and
determination to the challenge of every problem. But this afternoon she'd been intimidated.
Instead of answering that boor in his own sarcastic vein she'd let him get the best of her.

Why was she so elated, then? There was something about that man, she reflected, turning off
the Drive and heading for the quiet side street
where the Warren town house was. There was
something about that man that set her off balance. She recalled his huge, strong arms, the
broad expanse of his chest, and a primitive chill
shot through her. She'd never met a man like
that in her sheltered world. He looked like someone who'd knocked around the globe, just as her
grandfather had when he was young.

Erica smiled at the sight of Josh Warren's
house. It had an old-fashioned gaiety that always appealed to her; an architect had original-
ly designed it for his own use in 1912 and its
many shutters, wrought-iron balconies, dormer
windows and mansard roof gave it a lightness
that was a welcome relief beside the other pomp-
ous buildings on the block. Erica drove through
the porte cochere leading to a courtyard and
garage in the rear. She sat for a moment at the
wheel of the car and remembered how it had felt
when she was pulled out of the water—those
hard, strong hands touching her breasts in such
an impersonal way, as if she were no more than

a bale of cargo. Most of all she was haunted by the startling color of the dark stranger's eyes. They were so light a gray they looked like silver —like "silver fire."

Erica shook her head. She couldn't go on dreaming; her clothes were sodden and her head had begun to ache. She fervently hoped she wouldn't run into her aunt, who shared the town house with her as a "chaperone," a word that people hardly even knew anymore, much less used. She could picture her aunt's elevated brows and imagine her acid comments.

But as bad luck would have it Meredith Blaine was in. Erica heard her call out from the "drawing room," as her aunt still styled it. Trying to escape upstairs, Erica was arrested by the repeated sound of her name.

"Good heavens, my dear. What's happened to you now?" Erica's stately aunt was standing in the doorway, examining her with disapproving gray eyes. "Have you had an accident? I told you not to buy such a heavy car."

"It couldn't be the car, Merry dear." Disconcerted, Erica heard the drawling voice of her cousin George, Meredith Blaine's son. Then she saw him, standing a little behind his mother. Of all days for George to visit, Erica thought, this was the most disastrous. His lazy drawl was as misleading as his mother's nickname, which could never have been appropriate even when she was a child.

George looked amused, delighted to catch Erica out, to be one up in their continuing feud. He owned only ten percent of Warren stock in contrast to Erica's forty-nine and had never ceased to resent it.

"She's only wet, Merry darling, not wounded. I say, Erica, where *did* you go to lunch? The Aquarium?"

"Coney Island," Erica retorted. "We fished for it."

"Well, go upstairs at once and attend to yourself." Her aunt's tone recalled a hundred similar occasions, from scraped knees to childish fights with George and Roger and late returns from parties.

"I was trying to." Erica's smile belied her impudent answer; she liked Merry and could never understand how she could have given birth to someone like George. Merry Blaine shook her head with its sculptured gray hair, and a smile twitched at the corners of her stern mouth. George saw the smile and frowned.

"When you look human come down and have tea with us."

"All right." Erica spoke without enthusiasm. She ran up the curving stairs. She would have to think up a story for her aunt; Merry would pass out if she knew a strange man had put his hands on her niece's "bosom" and seen so much of her long legs. The 1980s had arrived without Merry's consent; she abhorred their music, manners and dress. Yet surprisingly she was an ardent feminist. At fifty-five her views on women's rights were even more advanced than Erica's.

When Merry's husband, the late John Philip Blaine, had abandoned the Stock Exchange for advertising and frequent business with fashion models, she had never forgiven him. Her favorite son, Jack, had died in the war; she was left with only the effete Roger, who took to the stage, and the disappointing wastrel, George, who took over his father's business. That business was already in difficulties; the clear-sighted Merry understood why her brother Josh had left Warren to Erica instead of to George and Roger.

Merry's own position was secure. Josh had said frankly in his outrageous will that his sister would need his money with George at the helm of Bradburn and Blaine. Josh left his sister a respectable number of preferred shares in Warren's and a handsome cash bequest, with the proviso that none of it be invested in Bradburn and Blaine or in Roger and George.

Erica hurried into her bedroom, shut the door and stripped off the muddy dress. It might revive with a cleaning. She hung it in the bathroom to dry, along with her fragile bra. She tossed the ripped pantyhose into a shell-shaped wastebasket.

Thoughtfully Erica examined her naked body in the mirrored wall. She approved of what she saw. She ran her hands over her breasts; they were surprisingly full for someone so slim and her hips were slenderly rounded. Her skin felt satiny under her fingertips. Erica's body tingled; she imagined the hands of the dark swimmer on her bare flesh. She was surprised at herself. Neither Morgan nor any other man had ever made her picture that with such vividness.

Then Erica's brown gaze crept upward from

her body's mirrored image with its long, slender legs to study her face and hair. She laughed. She looked like a child who'd been making mud pies.

"And he saw me like *this*," she whispered. What an idiot she must have looked, holding out her hand in that social manner, with a black stain of river mud on her upper lip like a comical moustache. No wonder he'd made fun of her. Taking off her watch and bracelet she ran steaming water into a big turquoise tub, shaped like a shell, and sprinkled the water liberally with carnation-scented bubble bath. Sinking into the blue froth she lay back and relaxed from head to toe, absently soaping herself, feeling the nerve knots loosen.

But something about the foaming caress of the bubbles conjured up the same sensations she had felt a few minutes before. Letting out a mild groan, Erica finished bathing and got out of the tub, drying herself on a fluffy blue-and-green towel. Her annoyance increased; everything reminded her of that man's hands.

She wandered disconsolately into the bedroom. Maybe her friends were right; she wasn't very "now." She hadn't been around enough; she'd had too little experience with men for someone her age or she'd never be reacting so strongly to that encounter. Yet something had always held her back. Her dedication to a career had not been a reason—it had been an excuse, she realized now. An excuse for clinging to her dream of one wonderful man who could fulfill her.

She sat down at her dresser and looked at her

face. Her color was high, almost feverish, and her eyes looked huge, vulnerable and soft. It was an expression her aunt would easily be able to read.

With an artful hand she made herself up lightly, but paid special attention to her eyes. With shadow she contrived to make her lids seem to droop languorously; she looked less excited, less open this way. Erica put on a little more lipstick than usual, but it only brought out the feverish spots of color in her usually pale high-boned cheeks. She gave up, sighing.

She heard a light tap at the door and slipped on a robe, calling, "Come in."

Her aunt entered and stared at her critically. She crossed the room and put an inquiring hand on her niece's face. "I think you have a fever."

Erica moved away. "No, darling, I don't have a fever." After an instant she asked casually, "Is George still here?"

"No, he's gone. We gave you up." Merry examined her again. "What happened to you today?" She sat down on a pouf near the dresser.

"The silliest thing . . . when we were going into Sweets a fireplug burst or something and drenched us." Erica turned away to hide her expression, making an elaborate show of winding her watch. She was never any good at lying, especially to her aunt.

"That's interesting," Merry remarked in a skeptical way. "I never noticed a fireplug there." Her voice was very dry. "Are you going out with Morgan tonight?"

"Yes."

"You don't sound too thrilled. He's a nice young man, as men go. He wouldn't make a bad husband." Erica was silent. "I'm hoping," Merry continued, "he'll have a good influence on George."

Erica ignored her aunt's comments. "You know," she said with an air of surprise, "I still haven't had lunch."

Distracted, Merry said, "You're impossible, child. You're skin and bone now. I'll get Hattie to bring you something this minute." She got up and bustled out.

Sighing with relief, Erica lay down on her chaise longue and closed her eyes. She drifted into a half-sleep, partly dreaming, partly imagining that she and the dark stranger were sailing off together on the *Sereia de Madeira* toward an uncharted horizon.

Morgan had said, "Dress up." Perversely, knowing that he disliked pants, Erica had chosen a new pants outfit of panne velvet—a romantic, lighthearted ensemble, but the least revealing thing she owned. It consisted of a billowy tunic with a jeweled belt over soft, wide trousers. Her vivid hair was smoothed back and she wore large dangling earrings of red-gold. The russet, green and gold mélange of the velvet was stunning with her hair and she enjoyed the free, clownish feeling of the ensemble.

Hurrying out of the restaurant with Morgan, Erica grinned.

"What's so funny?" he demanded. He was still in a bad mood, she realized, because of her cool manner in the intimate candlelit room.

"Oh, nothing," she murmured, remembering her aunt's reaction to her outfit. "Good heavens!" Merry had cried, seeing her descend the stairs at home. "What is that outlandish thing? You look like Emmett Kelly with earrings."

Morgan had reacted to her clothes in much the same way, although he'd been too polite to put it as frankly as Merry had. He'd simply raised his brows and said stiffly, "You look . . . quite nice."

Now, to make matters worse, Morgan was irritated because they were late for the theater. When they hurried into the Vivian Beaumont Theater at Lincoln Center it was almost curtain time.

Erica brushed against another latecomer—a tall, strong man in a brown suede suit. She murmured an apology.

"Quite all right."

The man had a rough, angry manner. He stood aside abruptly to let her pass. She glanced up at his face.

It was the man from the clipper. For an instant his silver gaze held hers and there was a glint of something like amusement in his eyes as they swept her boldly from head to foot. His glance was almost the same as it had been that afternoon when it took in her sodden, muddy clothes and bedraggled hair.

Erica felt a sudden jolt of excitement so strong that she almost felt her body sway with it; the excitement was quickly followed by resentment.

How dare he look at her like that, as if she had been put on earth for nothing but his amusement?

She stared back at him belligerently, then moved on. In the last-minute confusion Morgan, who had become separated from her, returned to her side and they took their seats. From his matter-of-fact expression Erica gathered that he hadn't seen the other man.

Morgan handed her a program and, as he read his, remarked, "This actor's a friend of Roger's, isn't he?"

"Which one?" Erica asked absently, catching sight of the familiar dark head several rows ahead of them on the other side of the aisle.

"This one," Morgan said a little irritably, pointing at the program.

"Oh. Oh, yes, I think so."

Next to the dark head, which looked smoother and more civilized tonight, was a sleek feminine head of dazzling blondness; when the blond head leaned in an intimate way toward the dark one, Erica recognized the woman. It was Arabella Loving, one of the most notorious jet-setters in New York. Her parties, which Erica avoided, featured too much liquor and too many people who seemed to have no sense of morals whatsoever. Arabella had recently obtained a divorce, but her carryings-on had been no less wild before.

Erica's heart sank. So that was the kind of woman he preferred. And she asked herself why it should matter to her; he was a rude, unpleasant man she'd met twice in passing and would probably never meet again. But at the same time she felt her heart pounding uncomfortably; the palms of her hands were moist and she was overpowered by the same primitive excitement that she had experienced that afternoon when his hard, rough hands had grasped her body. She took a long shuddering breath. Morgan glanced at her quizzically and she turned her head away from him.

Then she heard a woman behind her whisper, "My dear, look what Arabella's bought *now*."

"*Bought!* Don't you know who that *is*?"

Erica waited, breathless, for the first woman's answer as the houselights dimmed.

At last the second woman whispered, "My dear, that's Steven *Kimball*."

Chapter Two

Steven Kimball.

Erica was so astonished that she hardly realized the play had started; everything before her was a blur. She wondered if she'd involuntarily repeated the name because Morgan, who was leaning intimately toward her, made a restless movement. But when she glanced at him he was watching the stage.

She had been pulled out of the harbor by Steven Kimball, the phenomenal head of Warren's giant counterpart, Kimco. "Mr. Mask" himself. Kimball had co-founded his own company before he was twenty, declaring that he would be a multimillionaire in ten years. According to all reports, he had become one. Erica had always wanted to meet him, just because it would be so stimulating to talk with a man who'd gone so far while still so young and still kept two things she envied him—his privacy and an utterly outrageous manner of dealing with the world of business. But he kept such a low profile that he was almost invisible. Few photos had ever been taken of him. Those which had were smudgy and distant; no wonder he had looked familiar to her and to Morgan and yet was unidentifiable. The frustrated press called him "Mr. Mask."

Stories on him in the major newsmagazines showed a photo of him at age twelve; his impervious public relations men were under orders to release nothing more recent. Very little moved or impressed Steven Kimball, apparently. Erica smiled in the dimness, remembering the magazine that had gone to press with a sketch of the pre-teen on its cover. His addresses were a deep secret, but the staggering variety of his holdings was not. They ranged from tractors to cosmetics, from missiles to jeans to publishing houses. He rarely appeared on the Stock Exchange, usually sending representatives. Erica admired and envied him. She'd often dreamed of making Warren's as diversified as Kimco.

Now, she thought, absently hearing the clear, carrying voices of the actors onstage, she'd met Steven Kimball in the fetid waters of New York harbor with grime on her face. She still couldn't believe it.

The play dragged on; the audience was swept by laughter and she could feel the vibration of Morgan's answering laugh with his shoulder near hers. She felt him glance at her in surprise; she hadn't responded to the comedy at all and her sense of humor was generally quick and ready. She was always about to bubble with laughter. She made herself smile simply to divert Morgan.

At last the curtains closed for intermission and Morgan asked her, smiling, "Shall we?"

"Oh, yes, of course," she stammered and rose.

As they were making their way to the lobby Erica came almost face-to-face with Steven Kimball.

"Well, I'll be—" She heard Morgan's low exclamation behind her. She glanced back over her shoulder; his face was like a thundercloud.

For a brief moment Kimball stared straight into her eyes. She saw a look of great brightness in those strange silver irises and her heart hammered against her ribs. It was an almost painful sensation and she couldn't quite get her breath. Then the moment passed and the impetus of the moving crowd urged them all politely forward.

Erica watched Kimball and his blond companion walking up the aisle—Kimball's strong, immaculate hand carelessly grazing Arabella Loving's satiny, tanned waist, quite bare over the swooping back line of her dress. It had almost no top.

Suddenly Erica hated her own covered-up ensemble. Her figure was ten times better than Arabella's. She recalled with a pang how Merry had compared her to Emmett Kelly, the famous clown. And irrationally she felt like a waif in too-big hand-me-downs. Worst of all, she had a wild desire for Kimball to touch her as he was touching Arabella. She was so uneasy that by the time they got to the lobby she felt as if her face were burning up.

Morgan commented, lighting his cigarette, "Arabella's a bigger fool than I thought, to pick up a character like that."

So Morgan still hadn't recognized him. For an instant amusement overcame Erica's discomfort. She murmured, "Well, I don't know. She *is* very aptly named."

Morgan looked surprised. It wasn't like her to make catty remarks, but he grinned appreciatively. "Indeed she is." Then he stared at Erica's face. "You look flushed, darling. Do you think you're getting sick from that drenching today?"

"I do have a bit of a headache," she admitted, glad to have an excuse for her trembling voice and high color. "I'll go take an aspirin in the powder room if you'll excuse me a minute."

"Of course." He examined her with a worried expression.

She hurried off, thinking miserably: He didn't seem like that this afternoon—like a man who would run with Arabella's crowd. But he must be like all the rest, the men who looked on sex as a kind of handshake. She felt a crazy disappointment, a kind of sick feeling, picturing Steven Kimball with Arabella.

She didn't stop at the powder room; looking back, she saw that Morgan had turned away and was talking to a broker they both knew. Erica went out one of the exit doors that led to Lincoln Center's great central pavilion.

She took a grateful breath of cooling air and wandered toward the illuminated fountain in the center of the complex, before the Opera House. There were few people walking in the pavilion, for the air had turned unseasonably cool; Erica stood for a moment drinking in the refreshing moisture.

Through the leaping fronds of light and water she caught sight of a tall and solitary man with a powerful body and thick black hair. It was Steven Kimball. He was staring at the water, too, and evidently had not seen her. His face looked blank and lonely. Then he saw her.

"Good evening," he called out.

She didn't answer; her throat felt tight, as if it were closing up.

He walked around the big circular fountain and stopped a few feet away, staring at her.

She found her voice and was surprised at how calm she sounded when she said, "Good evening, Mr. Kimball."

He was silent, still looking at her. He showed no particular reaction to her calling him by name.

Despite herself she felt uneasy again, overwhelmed by his tall presence. The beauty of the night and the leaping bright fountain were a perfect setting for magical occurrences, unforgettable words. She hoped suddenly, with all her heart, that he would say such words, say something to her that would dignify this lovely place, make them both forget the absurdity of their first meeting.

His silver gaze swept over her face and hair and the velvet clothes whose rich autumnal colors glowed in the fountain light. Breathlessly she waited for what he would say.

"You're much too pretty to be dunked tonight. I hope you won't dance on the edge of the fountain."

The words jarred her, breaking the spell. First she felt a foolish hurt; then she was warmed by healthy anger. How could he? He was the nastiest man she'd ever met. He talked to her as if she were an adolescent, not a full-grown woman. A woman, in fact, with spunk enough to run one of the biggest conglomerates in the nation. Damn Steven Kimball.

"Not tonight," she retorted coolly. "I'm surprised that Arabella's not here, though. I know she likes skinny-dipping."

He raised his black swooping brows. "You know Arabella?"

"Not as intimately as you, I'm sure," she blurted and immediately felt like a fool. What on earth had possessed her to say such an idiotic thing?

Kimball smiled and his smile was not pleasant. He looked arrogant and pleased with himself; his strange eyes gleamed. "You seem to know a great deal about me."

Her heart sank. She was not only miserably embarrassed to have made such a personal comment to a stranger, but his last words were a tacit admission that he was close to the flagrant Arabella. Erica took a quick, deep breath to steady her voice.

"Only what others know," she said coolly. "Mostly what you looked like at twelve . . . and now that you have the manners of a twelve-year-old, too."

She was gratified to see his nettled expression. At the same time it was difficult not to respond to his extraordinary attraction; he fairly exuded strong, unashamed masculinity. There was nothing "liberated" about Steven Kimball, she reflected. He looked like a man from a heartier era; again, his likeness to a pirate struck her, setting her off balance as it had that afternoon at the harbor.

"Then it seems I have the advantage of you, Miss Warren."

He knew who she was, then. He must have known this afternoon.

"Not only am I your senior," he added, smiling his maddening smile, "because you acted like a ten-year-old this afternoon—" She exclaimed angrily, but he went on as if he hadn't heard, "but the exploits of the 'Baby Tycoon' are known to everybody. Perhaps you'd like me to recommend a better p.r. man." He laughed.

Her face felt hot again and she was too annoyed to find a ready retort.

"You really shouldn't let the media exploit you like that. And you should find an escort who can keep you out of the water." He grinned wickedly. His grin made him look more piratical than ever and she was irritated to find herself responding to it.

"I trust you're not offering your services?" she asked scornfully.

"Heaven forbid. I'm much too afraid of your fancy friend." His own contempt was all too plain. "Where is he, by the way? Does he think it's safe to let you get this close to the fountain?"

She was furious now. He was surely the rudest, most obnoxious man she'd ever met. But she wasn't going to act the way she had this afternoon. She'd match him insult for insult if it was the last thing she ever did. "And what about your date?" she countered. "Does she think it's safe to go out with a man who hates women so much?"

For an instant there was a strange look in his bright, piercing eyes; she thought she'd hit home. But at once his expression was blank again, amused. He laughed. "Arabella? She's not afraid of the devil himself. But you are, Miss Warren, and that's a pity. I think you're afraid to be yourself. And I think you're afraid of real men."

Erica spluttered. She was almost speechless at this attack, as well as the slur on Morgan's manhood. Steven Kimball was worse than she had imagined; he was not only rude, he was downright brutal.

I won't stand here another moment, she resolved. I should have walked away a long time ago. Why she hadn't mystified her. Then a taunting voice inside her answered: It's not so mysterious, after all. This is the most attractive man you've ever met in your life. That's the answer, nothing else.

She thought for one terrible moment that she might burst into tears and that would never do. It would give this boor too much satisfaction. "I don't know what your problem is, Mr. Kimball, and I don't want to know."

She turned away and hurried back toward the tall columned building where the theatergoers were streaming from the balcony back inside. She was going to be late for the curtain.

"I know yours, my dear lady," his insinuating voice followed her. "They don't call you the 'Ice Princess' for nothing."

Erica winced. The other nickname the gossip columnists had given her, indicating her old-fashioned austerity, sounded more unpleasant than ever in Kimball's rough, heavy voice. To her exasperation, in her haste she stepped right out of one of her strapless slippers.

She heard his laugh behind her. Before she could retrieve her shoe Kimball was beside her, stooping down to pick up the small copper-colored shoe and slip it on her stockinged foot.

"You need a keeper," he commented. His voice had a contemptuous ring. It irritated her, shamed her, that the voice, even while it ridiculed her, was the most exciting sound she'd ever heard. It affected her like ruthless, imagined hands on her secret skin. She had to get away; she couldn't stand being near this man another second. Without another word she went on, not looking back, and hurried into the theater.

The lights were already dimming again when Erica excused herself and slipped into the seat beside Morgan.

"How's your headache?" he whispered, looking at her curiously. "You got lost."

"Much better," she whispered back, ignoring his other comment. The play had begun again when she saw, out of the corner of her eye, that Steven Kimball was walking unconcernedly back to his place. He seemed in no hurry at all.

Erica thought savagely: He has as little consideration for anyone as he had for me. His reference to the "Ice Princess" still rankled. Then it annoyed her even more that she had taken his comments so personally. When Morgan took her hand she left it in his grasp. And when the curtain fell and the lights came up she delighted him with a warm, brilliant smile.

Feeling Kimball's glance on her, Erica defiantly took Morgan's arm and looked up at him with an openly tender expression.

Morgan was so surprised at her unexpected warmth that he kept his gaze on her all the way up the aisle until he paused to light a cigarette.

Before they could move away she heard a brassy feminine voice, hard and clear, calling out in an affected accent, "Well, well. Who have we here? Morgan and Erica."

Erica turned. Arabella Loving was smiling at them broadly. "How did you like the play? Wasn't it fun?"

"Oh, yes, great fun." Erica felt like adding, "I suppose," since she had hardly seen it at all. She noticed two things at once: Morgan had a rather annoyed, chagrined expression; Steven Kimball was standing behind Arabella, taking them all in with a blank face.

"Aren't you speaking to me, Morgan?" Arabella asked brightly.

"How are you, Arabella?" Morgan returned coolly, studiously ignoring her companion.

"But I don't think you two have met Steve," Arabella said. "Steven Kimball. Miss Warren, Mr. Hunt."

"We've met," Erica murmured sweetly, giving Kimball a cool half-smile. Then she glanced at Morgan. His face was a study; she nearly laughed out loud. His amazement was obvious; he was as astonished as she had been to find out who the rude seaman was.

But Morgan recovered himself swiftly and said a cold how-do-you-do to Steven Kimball. "Yes, we've all met before," he said ironically. "Under very unusual circumstances." He shot a hostile glance at Kimball.

"Very unusual," Kimball agreed, grinning at Erica.

"I had no idea. How mysterious you sound." Arabella looked at their faces with eager curiosity. "Why don't we all have a drink together?"

"Thank you, no," Erica said quickly, just as Morgan rushed into speech with, "We have other plans."

"I have an early day tomorrow," Erica concluded awkwardly, speaking over Morgan.

"Well, don't all of you rush to accept at once."

Arabella laughed harshly. "I forgot our little Erica's one of the laboring classes."

Torn between irritation and amusement, Erica thought: She makes me sound like one of the sweatshop girls from the old days.

"Unfortunately, we all are, Arabella." Kimball spoke abruptly. "Perhaps we'd better get going. Nice to see you again, Miss Warren, Mr. Hunt." He nodded briefly and took Arabella's elbow, urging her toward the entrance.

Erica heard Arabella asking Kimball, "Where on earth did you run into *her*, darling?"

"Let's go," Morgan growled and they went out of the theater into the pavilion.

Kimball and Arabella had already disappeared. The fiery fountain still leaped in the dark and Erica recalled the strange encounter of an hour before.

They passed by the illuminated circle but Morgan did not give it a glance; his gaze was on Erica.

"You didn't look very surprised when Arabella introduced us," he commented. "Good heavens. Steven Kimball. And I offered him money this afternoon." He laughed sardonically. "He must have gotten a kick out of that . . . making such a monkey out of me."

When she didn't answer, he said, "You knew who he was, didn't you? How in the devil did you know? You never said a word to me."

"The subject didn't arise," she answered calmly. "I heard someone behind me at the theater talking about him."

"I see." Morgan glanced at her curiously

again and took her arm before they went down the stairs to the street.

His dark-blue Bentley was parked a few feet away. He insisted on helping her in and, getting in on the other side, slammed the door and took her roughly in his arms.

"Erica." He pulled her face to his and kissed her—a hard, demanding kiss that took her completely by surprise. She regretted her earlier change of manner; it had been utterly childish to react warmly to Morgan just to put Steven Kimball in his place. She should have realized she'd have Morgan to deal with when they were alone and now it had already begun.

She pulled away and he said angrily, "What's the matter with you, Erica? One minute you're cold as ice, and the next minute you're"—he paused delicately—"not."

She didn't answer. His sudden advance had shaken her more than she cared to admit—not because of the kiss itself. He'd kissed her before. But because his touch reminded her of the touch of Steven Kimball. The man's very voice had affected her more than Morgan's kiss. She felt a terrible confusion, an inner trembling.

Morgan started the car angrily and the Bentley shot downtown; he made a sudden, savage turn, heading east.

"Please don't drive like that," she ordered in a cold voice.

He slowed down at once and muttered, "I'm sorry, Erica. It's just that you get me so . . . you make me crazy sometimes."

"*I'm* sorry for that," she said, and meant it. "I

don't know what's the matter with me. I guess I'm . . . working too hard," she concluded weakly.

"Amen to that," he said and smiled, but he kept his eyes on the road. "That's exactly what I want to talk to you about. Why don't we go somewhere quiet and have a nightcap?"

"I really can't," she said, forcing reluctance into her voice. "I *do* have an early day tomorrow, you know."

She knew that she had offended him again, for he replied curtly, "Very well." He did not speak again during the drive uptown.

But when he pulled up in front of the Warren town house he said, "Surely you can invite me in for one drink. I have to talk to you."

She hesitated, then said, "Of course."

Erica let them in with her key and, tossing her small bag onto a hall table, went into the big living room, going about to turn on several lamps.

"Oh, what a shame," Morgan said softly. "The dim light was nice." She knew that ingratiating tone; he was leading up to something again.

Without answering she went to a sideboard and asked in a neutral voice, "What would you like?"

"To marry you, of course. The same thing I've been wanting for the past three years."

Patiently she repeated, "What will you drink?"

"Scotch, please." She poured his drink over ice and took a small glass of sherry for herself, less because she actually wanted it than to have something to occupy her hands. She handed him his drink and sat down in an armchair.

He looked at the couch and said softly, "Sit by me."

"I'm too comfortable to move." Her answer was evasive.

"Erica." He set down his glass on the marble table before the couch and strode toward her. Gently he took her goblet from her fingers and set it on the round mahogany table by her chair. "No more fencing. Please."

She looked up at him and saw a determined expression on his handsome face, a brightness in his blue eyes.

He took her hand and drew her upward from the chair until she stood facing him. Then he put his arms around her and held her close, speaking against her hair. She only came up to his chin; he was very tall. She could feel the heat of his breath on the top of her head and she disliked the sensation.

Steven Kimball was even taller. The thought came from nowhere to disturb her even more. Morgan didn't even hold her in a very decisive fashion, she concluded. She moved restlessly in his grasp; he tightened his hold.

"Please," he whispered. "Don't keep running away. You know I love you . . . that I'll take care of you. For the last time, when are you going to marry me?"

She moved out of his grasp then and looked up at him. "The last time, Morgan? Is that a promise?"

She saw that he was restraining himself with difficulty; her pert question had unsettled him. "I won't give up, if that's what you mean."

Erica went back to the chair. She sat down and picked up her sherry, sipping it.

"I've told you no before," she said quietly, "but you've never believed me."

"Because I think you don't know what's good for you," he retorted and sat down on the couch near her chair.

"And you are?"

"I know I am," he asserted complacently. "You need me, Erica. A woman with a husband is in a much better bargaining position with the board, for one thing."

"Are we talking about marriage or a merger?" she asked, amused despite herself.

"I'm not joking," he said in a serious way. "Warren's is too much for you, too much for any young woman. You need advice and guidance; you needed it badly before you jumped into this 'Erin' thing."

"I have advisers," she reminded him coolly, "and they were all wrong about the Erin Division." Erin was the new subsidiary she had created over the protests of the board; its name combined her first and last names. It was the first of Warren Industries' glamour endeavors, devoted to fashion. She had undercapitalized it from the beginning, due to board opposition, and had to admit that she was running into difficulties. But the division was her special pet and she resented Morgan's comments.

"George says Erin's in trouble," Morgan said.

"You're in very close touch with George, it seems. I'm surprised you don't know Arabella Loving better. He talks of almost no one else."

She was puzzled by his reaction; he turned beet-red and she wondered why.

"We're not discussing Arabella. Or George. I'm talking about you."

"It seems to me we're talking business," she retorted. She set down her glass and rose. "I'm sorry, Morgan. You'll have to forgive me. I'm very sleepy."

He put his own glass down on the table with a sharp sound and got up hastily. "Erica, stop this. I didn't mean for this discussion to degenerate into a . . . quarrel."

"I'm not quarreling, Morgan. As for the other matter, I'd like to save us both a lot of trouble. I can't marry you. Not now, not ever."

"Erica, you can't mean that." He looked genuinely dismayed and she felt a little sorry for him. But it was impossible. She could never marry a man she didn't love and it was all too plain now that she could never love Morgan Hunt. She had tried to give it a chance, but there was no use any longer.

"Give me a chance," he begged her. "I can make you love me, Erica."

She shook her head. "Oh, no, Morgan. If it's not there the first moment it will never come. I was foolish to think otherwise."

"That's romantic nonsense. It's nothing to base a marriage on," he protested.

"There's nothing else to base a marriage on." She looked at him steadily and saw his blue gaze waver. But he had that determined, bullheaded look she'd seen a hundred times before.

"No, you're wrong. And I'll prove it."

"You won't have a chance, Morgan. I'm not going to see you again."

"Don't say that. Please don't say that." He put his hands on her shoulders and looked pleadingly down into her eyes.

"Morgan, I don't know what I can say to convince you. But I will not marry you."

He let his hands fall to his sides and released a long, weary breath. "All right, Erica. I won't badger you anymore tonight. But I'm telling you, I haven't given up. And I won't."

He kissed her cheek quickly and walked out of the room. With a sigh of relief she heard the front door close. She sat down in the big chair again and took another sip of the fine full-bodied sherry.

She'd been wrong; Steven Kimball was not the most exasperating man she'd ever met. Morgan was. If Steven Kimball had proposed to her he probably wouldn't have left at all until he got the right answer.

Steven Kimball . . . proposing? Erica suddenly laughed aloud at her own foolish fancies. A man like Kimball probably wouldn't propose to anyone, she reflected. Not if he enjoyed the company of women like Arabella.

And despite herself the thought of Kimball and Arabella, together, filled Erica with fresh anger and something like pain. She was going to put that man out of her mind, she determined. All men, for the moment. She had far too much to do to waste her time on speculation. And with quick resolve she got up and turned out the lights in the living room, going into the hall to extinguish the lamps there, then ran upstairs to prepare for bed. It was going to be a very long day tomorrow.

In for a penny, in for a pound, Steven Kimball reflected without humor as he followed Arabella Loving into the black-walled disco. When he'd told his friend Campbell, "I owe you one," he'd never thought it would mean getting stuck with Arabella for such a long night. But Campbell had called him yesterday morning, saying he had to fly to Amsterdam immediately. He'd made a date with Arabella for the theater and pub-crawling afterward.

The date was neither a casual nor a romantic one. Arabella was not just a pretty and free-spirited swinger. From her marriage she retained a share in Loving Metal and by birth she was Marshall Products. Both connections meant a lot to Campbell, and Campbell's connections meant something to Kimball, aside from their longtime friendship.

So here he was, "going public" for a change on the New York night scene. Not so public at that, he amended sardonically, fighting his way among the writhing dancers to get to a table in a pitch-black corner, as far as possible from the music. He'd never liked this music, even when he was a kid, and now it was worse than ever. The deafening noise almost rocked him backward.

Arabella, on the other hand, seemed buoyed by the horrendous racket; when the whirling red lights revolved, lighting her wild eyes and feverish face, she smiled at him brightly, rocking to the tuneless beat. Then she leaned forward with what he assumed was one of her come-hither poses and patted him on the chin.

He sat impassively under her touch, unsmiling, and thought how sad it was that she made him feel less than nothing. Poor silly woman. She removed her hand.

"What'll you have?" he bellowed over the pounding din.

"Scotch," she yelled, grinning.

He flagged a bikinied waitress, who started toward them, dodging dancers and milling drinkers like a commuter making the five o'clock dash at Grand Central.

She reached them a little breathlessly and as Steven shouted the order she gave him a seductive look. He didn't even glance at her as she undulated away, tottering on her needle-sharp heels, and it occurred to him for the hundredth time how unnatural it was: The more women took off, the less he reacted. Maybe that was one reason the Ice Princess had set him off, pulling at her dress that afternoon as if he'd never seen legs before. Showing up at the theater in that awful outfit that hid her from neck to ankles.

Steven smiled.

"What's the joke?" Arabella shrieked.

He shook his head. The girl came back with their drinks and he raised his glass to Arabella; she clinked her glass to his.

"Dance with me!" she yelled.

Resignedly he put down his glass and stood up, waiting for a squirming couple to move on before he followed Arabella onto the jammed dance floor. It was so crowded that they couldn't dance very far apart, which seemed to suit Arabella fine. She put her arms around his neck and moved close to him; he could feel all the contours of her body. This time Steven felt real dismay. Frenetic and useless as she was, Arabella Loving was a very seductive woman. And still here he stood, hardly able to get any closer to her, with no more reaction than a piece of lumber. He was hot with a strange, frustrated anger. Princess Warren had really gotten under his skin.

Suddenly the racket ceased; the comparative quiet was so loud it rang in his ears. It rocked him, and his head began to pound. Arabella walked close to his side as they went back to their table.

"How about a quieter place?" It seemed strange not to be shouting.

Arabella studied him, then said, "All right. If you like."

On the street he asked, "The Palm Court?"

She raised her brows. "Oh, honestly, you're stuffier than Morgan."

Suddenly his interest sharpened. "You're big buddies with Hunt?"

He flagged down a taxi. She laughed harshly while he helped her in and told the driver their destination.

Leaning back, he watched Arabella in the

flash of passing light. She had a pained and cynical expression.

"'Big buddies,'" she repeated in a rather slurred fashion. "You *destroy* me, darling. You're too delightful for words. Morgan Hunt is the coldest man in New York. How apropos that he chases the coldest woman." She laughed again, a little drunkenly, and her laughter had an unpleasant sound. Steven began to feel sorry for her. She sounded on the verge of weeping. He fervently hoped she wouldn't, though; she was hard enough to handle now.

"Ah, yes," she went on. "Even if little Erica wasn't Miss Money they'd still suit each other down to the ground. But I know something," she said mysteriously, giggling. "I know a little plot that Morgan's hatching with George."

"George?" Steven was fascinated now.

"George Blaine, sweetheart, the Ice Princess's own little cousin. Poor George, with his little ten percent. And Erica, with the 'Virgin Forty-nine.'"

Steven Kimball was quite aware that Erica Warren owned forty-nine percent of Warren's shares. But "virgin"? At the age of twenty-four —in these days of liberation? Now he was really surprised.

Arabella smiled at his expression. "Why, yes, my dear, Morgan and George are in cahoots. I thought you knew, Steve. I thought you knew everything that goes on on Wall Street. You're a card, darling, really you are. The very mention of money sharpens your teeth and brightens your eyes. Umm . . . what nice eyes you have. Give us a kiss."

She sounded really drunk now and Steven was having second thoughts about the Palm Court. "Perhaps we should give the Plaza a miss," he said casually.

"Oh, yes!" she cried. "You can come up to my place." She moved closer to him and put her head on his shoulder. She was almost asleep, he noticed.

He leaned forward and tapped on the plastic shield that separated them from the cabbie. Raising his voice, he gave the man the address of Arabella's penthouse apartment.

Then he leaned back. Arabella snuggled up to him and kissed his neck. "Umm . . . umm," she murmured, "a nightcap with Mr. Mask himself." She could hardly pronounce the words.

"We'll see," he said quietly.

Abruptly Arabella sat up, bumping his jaw with her sleek head. "What do you mean, 'we'll see'?" she demanded. "What's the matter with you? What's the matter with *me*?"

"Nothing's the matter with either one of us," he said gently. "Nothing in the world. But I've got a big day tomorrow and I've got to get some sleep. Besides," he added coaxingly, "I'm an old-fashioned guy. And I think you're hung up on Hunt."

"Yes. Yes, damn it, I'm in love with him." She started to cry. "And he doesn't care a thing for me at all. I'm all right for play, sure. But he'll keep chasing Erica till hell freezes over."

"Hey, take it easy." Her cheeks were wet, her

mascara and shadow a mess and she was sniffling. Steven took out a handkerchief and handed it to her. "Come on, now." She wiped her face. The cab was drawing up before her apartment house.

"Come up," she urged him. "At least we'll have fun. Love doesn't have anything to do with anything anymore."

He shook his head. "Sorry. Maybe another time," he lied. He told the driver to wait and walked Arabella to her lobby. When he got in the cab again, he thought, I'm probably a fool. What do I know about love? He'd never been in love with anybody in his whole life.

So Arabella was hung up on Morgan Hunt and Hunt was after Erica Warren. Or, more properly, Warren's, hand in glove with Blaine. It was an interesting situation. And it might make an even more interesting game, the kind that he, Steven Kimball, knew so well how to play.

It was like a little war, but Erica Warren, from what he'd seen of her, not to speak of what he already knew, would make a worthwhile opponent.

Chapter Three

*J*enny Landon, personal assistant to Erica Warren, sat down at her sleek, modern oak desk and opened her handbag. Quickly she checked her appearance in her pocket mirror. Her long blond ponytail was smooth and shining, her unmade-up face in order except for a tiny flake of soot she'd picked up somewhere on the way to work.

Then she eagerly attacked the morning mail; it had to be on Erica's desk when she came in at nine-thirty and only the priority mail belonged there. The rest Jenny could take care of herself with ease. She'd learned a lot in the three years she'd been with Erica Warren, first as her secretary, now as her personal assistant.

It was a title Jenny gloried in, just as she was thrilled by the big increase in pay that came with it. She had been given the title because the Erin Division idea had, in a way, come from her. Jenny delighted in remembering that. In fact, she delighted in everything about her work. The only cloud on her horizon was Paul's increasing jealousy of the job.

Jenny frowned. She wouldn't think about that at the moment. She had to concentrate on the mail. Determinedly she put the thought of her husband out of her mind and went through the letters. Taking the priority material into Erica's vast corner office, Jenny put the mail in the center of the curving desk, with phone messages on top, and returned to her own office.

As she sat down again the graceful swirl of her new Erin skirt gave her extraordinary pleasure. It was from the modestly priced Steal Collection, a wonderful blue-gray that matched her eyes and set off her skin and hair so well. Even Paul had to admit the outfit was "really something." The jacket was a soft, graceful cardigan style of tissue-weight wool that adapted marvelously to the varying temperatures of the city. Under the jacket this crisp morning Jenny wore one of the several coordinated tops—they came in a floral print, a stripe and a solid, which made the tops perfect mix mates for the other suit colors; Jenny had also gotten one in green, equally good with her blond coloring.

The outfit also came in sherry and claret for darker women. The clever design of the ensemble did amazing things for all sorts of figures—slimming the full, rounding the thin, making a sensation of the just-right.

Jenny was ahead of herself this morning; she had come in early, as she frequently did, and had a few pleasant moments to relax before getting together the papers for that day's board meeting. She picked up one of the fashion magazines set out invitingly in her sanctum and leafed through it to study the latest Erin spread.

A group of impossibly beautiful models, dressed in suits like Jenny's, were grouped in insolent poses around an impossibly handsome man dressed as a sheriff. The women's outfits were finished with cowboy hats, boots and mock gun belts. The whole colorful ad said nothing but "STEAL . . . from Erin."

Women were now so familiar with the Erin line that no more copy was needed. All the Erin clothes *were* a steal, combining imagination, beauty and quality tailoring with reasonable prices, something that the company had told Erica Warren was impossible. But she'd achieved the impossible—so far, anyway. Jenny sighed. She in fact had identified herself so closely with Erica's concerns that the imminent board meeting, which promised to be a difficult one, had her worried, too.

The addition of the Buccaneer and Rogue

lines—the latter for older women—had strained the precariously financed division and Jenny knew that Erica now needed more capital in the most urgent way.

Jenny Landon, in the last three years, had become more than an employee to Erica; they were now friends. Jenny knew a side of Erica Warren that the financial and gossip writers would never know—a vulnerable, generous and warmhearted woman who often seemed no older than Jenny's own twenty years.

Jenny glanced at the clock: nine-twenty. She deftly assembled the report for the board. As she was finishing, Erica came in. She was severely dressed today in a simple suit of turquoise and a ruffled silk blouse of deep brown with tiny turquoise dots. Her hair was smoothed back and she wore no jewelry except some small button earrings. She was beautiful, as always, but Jenny was dismayed to see dark circles under her wide brown eyes, as if she hadn't slept well. She looked tense.

"Good morning!" Jenny smiled, cheerful and enthusiastic as usual.

"Good morning. All squared away?" Erica's half-smile mirrored a certain apprehension. Jenny knew very well that she wasn't looking forward to the board meeting at eleven.

"All square," Jenny said reassuringly.

"Good. I hate to do this to you, but I have a few amendments to the report. I'll dictate them as soon as I've glanced at the mail. Think you can take care of it by ten forty-five?"

"Sure."

"Wonderful. I'm *so* glad you're here, Jenny."

As Erica went into her office, leaving the door ajar, Jenny felt warmly gratified and, oddly, protective and compassionate. She immediately laughed at herself for that. Erica Warren was the "girl who had everything," and yet sometimes Jenny had had the feeling her employer envied *her*. Envied Jenny her marriage and her love for Paul. It was the strangest thing. Not much to envy now, she thought sadly.

"Would you come in now, Jenny? Bring your book," Erica called out in the easy, friendly way she always had when they were alone.

"Coming." Jenny rose at once, taking her pad and pen, and went into Erica's office.

Erica felt her usual pleasure and approval when she saw Jenny come in and take the chair beside her desk. The girl's blue eyes were clear and bright, her rosy skin smooth and rested-looking.

Not for the first time Erica felt a pang of envy; Jenny always had such an aura of well-being and happiness, the look of a woman who was loved. Erica recalled her own restless tossing of the night before. She had been unable to get Steven Kimball out of her head; she'd slept poorly and knew it showed.

She pulled herself together and began to dictate from the notes she'd taken from her briefcase. Before Jenny left the office Erica said, indicating the correspondence, "We can do these this afternoon, even tomorrow. There's nothing pressing. After you rough that out and turn it over to the secretaries I'll take care of the calls. I'm sure you know the first order of the day." She smiled at Jenny.

"I certainly do," Jenny replied wryly.

As she was going out the door Erica commented, "You look great."

"Thanks." Jenny grinned and hurried back to her desk.

Erica rose and closed her door. She needed a little while to get herself together. This was going to be the toughest day she'd had in quite a while. Her usual energy and optimism had deserted her; she felt tired and distracted. And she'd need every ounce of her confidence to try to win them over.

She went to the minute kitchen adjoining her office, just off the small conference room, to get some coffee. She poured herself a cup of the strong black brew and wandered with it to the big boardroom beyond the small conference room. There was something particularly forbidding about it today—its long, shining walnut table and empty chairs. Erica shook her head, as if to throw off her apprehension, and took her coffee back to her desk. She sat down and sipped it, feeling a little more in command.

She let her mind wander backward a moment to the beginnings of Erin. The idea had come to her when she had heard Jenny complaining to another secretary about having so few clothes. "I just can't buy cheap," Jenny had declared.

"So I just buy few." Suddenly Erica had had a vision of quality clothes at a price more people could afford. When she planned the project and presented it to the board members they'd declared it to be "impossible" in these days of high production costs.

But the very word "impossible" was a challenge that Erica Warren felt obliged to meet. The word had never stopped Josh and it wouldn't stop her. The board scoffed, using the familiar phrases of "tight money," "killing interest rates" and "reckless expansion," pointing out that even a prestigious, highly capitalized hotel chain was drawing in its horns, deciding against additions to its properties.

Erica had listened and then gone off on her own. Using her own capital, a thing that Josh had warned her against, she bought up two failing dress houses. She fired them with her enthusiasm. The workers regained their craftsmen's pride; well-paid, they also enjoyed having a hand in making clothes "as good as they used to be." There was a startling, widespread ad campaign, for which Erica enlisted new, young and imaginative talent. Miraculously the division survived. There had been a thousand problems, but Erica had gloried in tackling every one, determined that Erin would succeed. She wanted it to be only the first of other such divisions.

But the board members had never recuperated from the shock of her "ill-advised action" in using her own capital; to them it was an indication of the reckless impulsiveness and poor judgment to be expected from a woman, especially such a young one. And now Erin was only breaking even; she had no soaring profit to show the board. Last month, it was true, the profits had increased a little, but without additional backing she might soon be in trouble. And she wanted to expand, with boutiques across the country. If she only had six more months she was confident of an upswing substantial enough to prove herself to the board.

Almost before she knew it Jenny was tapping at her door and entering with the freshly duplicated addenda. "Would you just glance at this?"

Erica took the sheet and rapidly scanned it. "Perfect. Thank you so much, Jenny." When her assistant had gone away Erica decided to make her calls, mostly of a routine nature, and scribble notes on the correspondence to keep herself busy before the anxious moment of the meeting with the board. To make matters worse, today she'd also be facing the hostile George and the resentful Morgan.

She held herself very erect, walking with a false spring to her step and forcing a smile to her lips as she entered the boardroom.

George and Morgan were already there, standing together at the end of the table near the great glass wall with its panoramic view of the harbor.

"Good morning," George drawled. He was

dressed, like Morgan, in the Wall Street western mode that most of the younger men affected, but he did not have Morgan's look of vigor. There was an air of dissipation about him that no amount of tanning could dispel, a raffish disorder that hinted at a late and active night. He was almost as tall as Morgan, but with a flabby look inappropriate to one so young; his mocking eyes, a travesty of Merry's clear gray ones, were bloodshot and pouchy.

"How is our little Erica?" he asked. Resentfully, she reflected that he sounded like an older boy allowing a little girl to play with his marbles, if she were careful enough with them.

"Excellent," she replied in a cool tone.

"Erica, how are you?" Morgan spoke to her in a tentative fashion, studying her face.

"Fine, Morgan," she answered him more gently. "And you?"

"As well as can be expected," he said in a meaningful way.

She was almost relieved when the other board members came in, but she noticed that two of them were missing. George and Morgan exchanged a glance; she had a feeling they knew something she didn't, that she was in for an unsettling surprise.

Her feeling of apprehension grew as the meeting was called to order and the chairman, a longtime associate of Josh's who disapproved of her thoroughly, said, "There is an item which I feel should be taken up at once, one which does not appear on the agenda. It is the resignation of two members of the board, Harlan Fane and Walter Madison—"

"May I ask," Erica interjected, "why I was not so informed?"

"Because, Miss Warren," the chairman said repressively, "the board itself was not informed until early this morning."

"The board?" she retorted. "Am I not still a member?" She could not keep the sarcasm out of her voice.

The chairman looked chagrined. "I beg your pardon. I should have said, certain members of the board."

"And the 'certain members' are . . . ?" Erica pursued.

"Myself, Mr. Hunt and Mr. Blaine. I regret that there was insufficient time to notify the other members."

Between nine and eleven? Erica thought skeptically. But she said nothing. She merely nodded, waiting.

"The stocks of Messrs. Fane and Madison," the chairman said in his old-fashioned way, "have been purchased by the Kimren Corporation, which has only today been listed on the Exchange."

"In other words, another toy of Kimco," George said lazily.

Kimco! Kimco was Steven Kimball. Erica felt a sharp dismay. Was Steven Kimball planning to take over Warren's? It couldn't be. Didn't he have enough? The man's greed was unbelievable.

Her thoughts must have shown on her face; George was staring at her, smiling.

"Please, Mr. Blaine." The chairman frowned. "You are out of order."

"I'm always out of order, Mr. Chairman," George said, unruffled. The chairman banged his gavel.

"This whole thing is highly irregular," the chairman said coldly. "But this is an unprecedented situation. The resignation of the members is explained in these letters." He handed copies around the table.

Erica read her copies and her heart sank; the members had resigned because of the matter of the Erin Division. But why, then, had Steven Kimball bought their stock if they had felt that Warren was being threatened? *Because he's planning a takeover,* she concluded. *And with his immense capital my little problems must seem like a piggy-bank matter.* She was getting furious.

The question of the resignations settled, the board members went on to the other items on the agenda. When they reached the Erin Division they showed themselves unalterably opposed to corporate capitalization of the project. The proxies created by the two members' resignation and transfer of their shares had cast their absentee votes with the conservative members of the board. George seemed to take a malicious delight in opposing Erica. Morgan, who did not meet her eyes, voted with George.

At last it was over. It was not until one o'clock that the chairman adjourned the session. When

Erica returned to her office Jenny stuck a tentative head around the doorframe.

"Oh, dear, I don't have to ask how it went."

"Is it as bad as that?" Erica asked wryly, leaning back in her chair.

"It never is," Jenny replied loyally. "But you don't look happy."

"I'm not. And we didn't get it."

"Oh, Erica, I'm sorry. What now?"

Erica smiled. "Bank-wards." Just thinking of the banks made her tired.

"Oh. Well . . ."

"Yes, indeed. You go on to lunch. I may be out most of the afternoon."

"Right. Good luck."

Erica picked up her bag and portfolio and left the office. Once the elevator had descended thirty floors and she was on the busy street she decided to take a walk before she got some lunch and faced the banks. Briskly she moved up Broadway toward City Hall Park. It would be nice, she reflected, to sit for a moment or two in the sun and watch the pigeons flying.

Some girl watchers, standing in the sun by a corner office building, whistled appreciatively when she passed. She ignored them but felt a little better in spite of herself. She crossed Broadway and walked into the sunlit park, not noticing a tall dark-haired man behind her. Erica sat down on a bench already occupied by a stately old man reading the paper and looked up at the Gothic commercial cathedral that was the Woolworth Building. Next to it a skyscraper was being constructed; she watched the orange-helmeted men at work up high, seeming to stroll along the narrow steel beams as blandly as if they were on the sidewalk, taking girders from the cranes like broad-armed dancers, graceful and slow.

Something in their daring and their muscularity reminded her of the maddening Steven Kimball and she felt again that primitive thrill she had experienced when he'd lifted her from the water and mocked her last night by the fiery fountain. And now he was going to meddle with her company.

Exasperated, she got up from the bench. Her momentary peace was shattered. She quickly crossed the street and went into Miller's.

She'd always liked the novelty of walking down from street level to find not a cozy bistro but a big, well-lighted conservative restaurant in the Woolworth Building's cellar. Erica had a delightful feeling of privacy there, of going practically unnoticed among the preoccupied judges and attorneys, well-known political figures and stately bankers.

That day, as usual, Miller's was crowded, the diners being mainly men. So again Erica, very preoccupied herself, still did not see the tall dark man who was almost on her heels.

Her calming sense of anonymity deepened when the rather harried hostess said quickly but politely, "There'll be a slight wait for a table, miss. You're alone?"

"No. We need two, miss." Erica heard the deep, growling voice behind her. Startled, she turned. Her eyes met a dazzling white shirtfront and a costly crimson tie printed with the minute figures of black buccaneers. She looked up; now she was staring into the silver eyes of Steven Kimball.

The hostess replied, "I'll let you know, sir," and rushed away.

"I didn't know we were together," Erica remarked ironically. Kimball was grinning from ear to ear, but she didn't smile back.

"We've been together, in a way, all the way uptown to the park," he retorted, still grinning. "Although we had separate benches there, admiring the new Kimball Building."

"I might have known. Do you own *everything*, Mr. Kimball? Is it really true that you've bought the Brooklyn Bridge and the Battery . . . is City Hall next?" She was so annoyed that she couldn't restrain her tongue.

"*Tsk, tsk,* Miss Warren." He raised his black brows in an expression of mock concern. "What a shrewish temper for such a lovely lady."

Erica tried to put some distance between them but an incoming party of three dignified-looking older men made it necessary for Steven Kimball to take a step forward, as if considerately making room were his only motive. But Erica felt him close behind her and her body prickled with a perverse excitement. He was so near that she could smell the clean musk of his body and the titillating scents of fine, light wool from his jacket and immaculate linen and a faint aroma of tobacco.

"May I?" he murmured, taking out a cigarette.

"Whatever you do is a matter of indifference to me," she said coldly.

"I'm crushed to hear it." He lit his cigarette. She noticed that he wore no cologne or shaving lotion. In spite of herself, she approved of that.

But she said coolly, half turning, "I'm having lunch alone, Mr. Kimball. I'm afraid you'll just have to wait."

"Have you no pity for a starving man, Erica?" To her discomfort he bent very near. She could feel his warm breath against her hair. "You really should have mentioned that to the hostess, you know. She's going to be very confused."

Erica was getting furious. Of all the unmitigated gall, she thought. At the same time, he had her there; she should have said something to the woman, and wondered why she hadn't. It was just because he'd taken her by surprise. That was it. Erica immediately felt better.

"I'll explain it to her, all right." She turned away from him again, scanning the smaller tables. Apparently, one was about to be vacated. Its solitary occupant, a City Hall man she recognized, was picking up his bill and putting down a tip.

The hostess signaled to Erica and Kimball, smiling. Erica went determinedly ahead, getting as far as she could in front of Steven Kimball, but his long strides caught up with her easily. "Thank you very much," he said to the hostess, putting a folded bill into her hand.

"Thank *you*, sir." The woman smiled brilliantly at Kimball and snapped her fingers at a passing waiter.

"Miss Warren." With great gallantry Steven Kimball pulled out a chair for her. Fuming, she sat down. There was no way out of it now, she supposed; she wasn't about to make a scene, because she'd sighted two brokers she knew, along with her grandfather's corporate attorney, at another table. They were all looking at her and Kimball with friendly interest.

Blast, she thought savagely. Now there'll be all kinds of gossip. Erica kept her face bland and neutral. When the waiter handed her a menu she buried herself in it, shielding herself against that piercing gaze.

"Peekaboo," he said in that rough, growling voice, and the combination of the voice and the foolish word threatened to make her burst into laughter. But she controlled herself sternly as Kimball peered around the corner of the menu at her. "Thank you very much for not making me starve," he added.

"It's really a pity," she retorted, "since this is the only restaurant in New York."

"It's the only one you're lunching in today," he returned, "and I wanted to talk to you."

"What about?" she asked ungraciously, putting down her menu. The waiter had returned.

"What will you have?" Steven asked.

She gave him her order and he transmitted both orders to the waiter.

"I wanted to apologize," he said when the man had gone. "And there are other matters."

"What other matters could there possibly be?" Her reply was frigid; she utterly ignored the comment about apologies.

"A great many. We have more in common than you can possibly know. I happen to know you've got certain problems."

"Really?" She managed to keep her voice calm, but she was thinking: So *that's* it. He's brought me here to pump me about Warren Industries. Her annoyance was succeeded by a sharp and irrational disappointment.

And she asked herself what she was doing there; she was so apprehensive about the afternoon that she had almost no appetite, anyway, and it would be utterly impossible to swallow anything in the company of this deceitful, sarcastic . . . boor.

Erica pushed back her chair, saying angrily, "If you're so hungry, Mr. Kimball, why don't you eat my lunch as well? First, you intruded on me. Now you have the nerve to use this meeting for a little industrial spying. Well, it won't work. Enjoy yourself."

She rushed out of the restaurant and hurried up to the street. Her head was aching from hunger and she felt a little foolish; now she'd have to face some difficult interviews on an empty stomach. But she couldn't have sat there a moment longer, under the circumstances. Most maddening of all was the memory of that quick, absurd disappointment when she realized that Steven Kimball had sought her out for business and not personal reasons.

On Broadway again, she squared her shoulders. It was time to face the banks. She headed downtown fast. In the lunchtime crowds Steven

Kimball, not far behind her, went totally unnoticed.

Kimball was curiously touched by the shoulder-squaring gesture. She was so little, he thought, to be carrying so much. She was a beautiful woman and no woman had ever affected him in quite the way she did. He had thrown a bill on the table as soon as she rushed off and followed her upstairs from Miller's. Now he recalled the real object of his quixotic chase and quickened his step. He saw her go into the imposing entrance of one of New York's largest banks.

She emerged with a discouraged face. He witnessed her entrance into two more banks. Then he stepped into a phone booth and made a quick, terse call.

Erica was dictating when Jenny took the call. "It's the president of Merchants Andover," Jenny whispered, covering the phone with her hand.

Amazed, Erica learned that the bank was interested in Warren's. She was flabbergasted, but said, "I'll be right over."

She hurried to Merchants Andover, a bank not noted for large investment loans, and was staggered to learn that the bank would lend her the money she needed. It had, she learned, a connection with a new government agency eager to back those investors who were bolstering the local economy by keeping business in the city, and it had been following Erin's progress for some time.

Elated, Erica concluded her business and hurried out to call Jenny. "Erin is saved," she said simply. "Can you give me an extra half-hour this evening? We have plans to make."

"You've got it," Jenny assured her.

It was after four when Erica got back to her office.

"You look reborn," Jenny said, smiling. Her desk was clear for a new project.

"I just was," Erica answered, grinning. She told Jenny what had happened. Then, glancing at her assistant's pristine desk top, she shook her head and commented admiringly, "You're too much, lady."

"What do you mean?"

"Your decks are clear already. And I couldn't have called more than ten minutes ago. What am I going to do without you on my scouting trip for the new boutiques?"

"You're going, then. When?"

"Next week."

"Wow! Soon." Jenny picked up her pad and pen, following Erica into her office.

"The sooner the better." Erica sat down at her desk, leaning back in her chair with a sigh of relief. "But you know how long I've been wanting to get started on the top ten—the other top ten, since we've got the Big Apple sewn up."

Jenny nodded, sitting in the chair by the desk. There were already six Erin boutiques in Manhattan, and one in Brooklyn, in addition to Erin

"Hideouts"—in keeping with the raffish bandit theme—in major department stores.

"Can I get you some coffee?" Jenny asked.

"Oh, yes, thanks. I need it. I'll bet you can use some, too."

"You are so right." Jenny disappeared briefly and returned with two steaming cups.

Erica took an appreciative sip of her coffee, then said briskly, "It's okay tonight? For you to stay, I mean. Paul's late night?" Jenny's husband, a student of interior design, usually had a late class on this evening, so Erica had no qualms about asking Jenny to work late.

"Yes, it's his late night, all right." There was an inflection in Jenny's voice Erica had never heard before—an angry, pained undertone. She studied her pretty assistant covertly but decided not to pursue the matter now; Jenny had her "shut" look and Erica felt that she might be intruding.

"Good," she said. "Now, about the tour. The top ten are listed in the back of my diary; here"—she picked up the handsome leather-covered book, with her name imprinted in gold leaf on the cover, from her desk—"although, knowing you, you probably already know them."

Jenny reeled off, "L.A., Chicago, Philadelphia, San Francisco, Detroit, Boston, Washington, Dallas, Miami, Houston."

"You amaze me. By heart, yet." Erica laughed with pleasure.

"But of course. And in geographical order—Boston, Philly, Washington, Miami, Detroit, Chicago, Dallas, Houston, San Francisco and L.A."

"I knew there was a reason why I made you my assistant. Now, get Shirlee"—Erica used the first name of New York's savviest travel agent—"and have her book the planes and give me a rundown on hotels. You know the kind of place I like." Jenny nodded once, smartly. She did: the kind of hotel that was luxurious but not flashy. "I've got some other things to look into."

It was almost ten minutes to six when Jenny had completed everything. But the job was perfectly, flawlessly done. The planes were booked; arrangements were made for company drivers to pick up Erica at the airports in the cities where Warren had subsidiaries; hotel reservations were made and Jenny had even gotten five-day weather forecasts which would help Erica choose the right clothes for the first two cities. Weather numbers, with area codes, were included for the other eight metropolises so she could phone ahead.

"You're a wonder," Erica told Jenny, looking over her memorandum.

"I want to be," Jenny said seriously. "This is the greatest job I've ever had in my life. I feel like I'm part of it. More than I'm a part of—" She stopped abruptly, flushing.

"A part of what, Jenny?" Erica asked in a gentle voice. "You know I never want to pry. But is something wrong at home?"

Jenny looked reluctant and embarrassed. "Yes, in a way. I was going to say, 'More than I'm a part of Paul's life.' "

"What's the matter?" Erica asked with concern. "You can tell me about it, you know."

"Sure I know." Jenny sounded grateful and warm. "You've just had . . . so much on you lately I didn't want to add to it, that's all."

"I'd like to know if there's any way I can help." Erica leaned over and took Jenny's hand.

"He's so unreasonable. But then, I guess artistic types always are."

"Yes, indeed," Erica said fervently, thinking of Roger. "Unreasonable in what way?"

"Well, he knows—besides the fact that I downright love this job—that we need the money." Erica nodded; it was no secret that Jenny and Paul lived on a tight budget. His part-time job, which allowed him sufficient time for school, brought in far less than Jenny's salary.

"And yet," Jenny continued resentfully, "when you made me your assistant and I got that wonderful raise"—she beamed—"he got all macho and started making remarks about being a kept man." Her beaming look disappeared and she frowned. "Yes, I know what you're too polite to say: He was a 'kept man' before, by his standards. He's just kept better now."

Erica smiled. "Well, I wasn't going to put it like that."

"You wouldn't, of course. *He* never put it that way before, but all of a sudden now he's terribly jealous of the job, jealous of the money I make. He . . . he calls me a moneygrubber and a cold-hearted career woman."

"Really," Erica said with indignation. "That's absurd. What if you *are* a career woman? Thousands of married women are and their husbands encourage them. These days a lot of families need two incomes . . . and women need fulfillment. Good heavens, my grandfather helped make me a career woman."

Erica paused, thinking: But am I a very good example . . . ? Married to Warren's instead of a man, the woman they call the Ice Princess?

She could almost see her own thoughts mirrored in Jenny's pretty eyes; there was a flicker of doubt there.

But Erica went on determinedly. "Jenny, you're made for a career. And since you don't, as you told me, plan to have children in the near future" (Jenny shook her head) "it's a criminal waste for you not to go as far as you can. I'm sure you know by now that I have bigger plans for you than being a mere assistant. There's almost no limit to how far you can go in the corporation. I think you're executive material."

Jenny stared at her excitedly; her blue eyes shone.

"I mean it. Your loyalty, your willingness to work . . . your brightness and imagination. Those are the qualities I want around me, the qualities I need to make Warren's bigger. Maybe even, someday, as big as Kimco." When she mentioned Kimball's giant conglomerate she couldn't hide a certain wistfulness. Quickly she looked down at the memorandum on her desk to hide the expression in her eyes.

When she looked up Jenny was studying her.

Resolutely she hurried on. "You know, I've almost been . . . jealous of you at times," she confessed. "Envious of your marriage. I've thought how nice it must be to go home to a husband." She smiled.

Jenny stared at her. *"You* envied *me?"* She added in amazement, "The lady who has everything?"

Erica made no comment, thinking: Not quite. Not quite everything.

"You know, before you told me this, Jenny, I was going to ask you if you'd like to make at least one part of the trip with me . . . at least to Boston and Philadelphia. You've always said you've never gotten to travel enough. But now . . . it would probably be a very bad idea. My grandfather once told me that a woman's greatest success is a good marriage. And there's something to that, despite all my protestations about careers. You and Paul have had a good marriage so far; maybe this is just a rocky time."

"I don't know. I just don't know. Oh, how I'd love to go with you." Jenny appeared to be going through a terrible inner struggle.

"Look, don't worry about it anymore tonight. Go home and relax." Erica got up, preparing to leave the office. "I'll call you from Boston on Monday."

Jenny was still sitting in her chair, indecisive, hesitant. Then she said, "Erica, could I . . . think it over and give you a call tomorrow? If I can go I can make all the arrangements with Shirlee from home."

"Of course. Let me know." Erica smiled and walked out of the office. Jenny was still sitting in the chair, her elbows on the desk. "Yes," she said quickly. "Tomorrow."

Jenny was too tired, after all that had happened that day and with the decision facing her that night, to take a bus or subway uptown to the Village. She hailed a cab, wincing at the sign announcing a new surcharge. Traffic was extremely heavy and she was starved by the time she got to Twelfth Street. She skipped the supermarket, aghast at the long lines at the checkout counter, and went straight home.

Their apartment was on the fourth floor of an old remodeled brownstone and generally she was delighted with it, despite the four steep flights—including the high stoop—she had to climb to reach it. She glanced at her watch; she couldn't believe it was nearly a quarter to eight.

Only an hour and forty-five minutes until Paul got home and she felt like she had everything in the world to do. For one thing she had to wash her hair, and he was running out of socks because he could never remember to pick up the laundry. Well, *she* wasn't going to, not tonight.

Jenny unlocked the door and entered their big, airy living room with its long, old-fashioned windows, the feature she most loved about the apartment. The place, however, was a mess right now. Paul, who left later than she did in the mornings, had plenty of time to pick up a few things, but never did.

Jenny sighed and went into the bedroom. The bed hadn't been made, either. She took off her Erin suit, hanging it carefully in the small closet. She put on a shirt and jeans and left her feet bare. She went to the kitchen for a hasty sandwich; she certainly didn't feel like cooking. Then she returned to the bedroom to make up the bed, hang Paul's unsoiled clothes in the closet, pick up his soiled things to toss in the hamper, straighten out her dresser and run a dry mop over the parquet floor.

In the kitchen she washed the breakfast dishes. Then, after a hasty straightening of the living room, she undressed again and took a long, hot shower, washing and blow-drying her hair.

By the time she'd slipped into an inexpensive but pretty nylon lounging dress and put on a little lipstick and mascara, she felt dizzy with tiredness. She had forgotten to check the mail. Putting on some slippers, she went cautiously down the three flights so she wouldn't slip and got the mail. The box was stuffed; she had to struggle to empty it. Back in the apartment she leafed through the mail; there were an awful lot of bills, it seemed. She just couldn't do anything with them now. She stacked the mail neatly on a side table and went into the bedroom, turning on the TV set.

It was already nine—only a half-hour left until Paul got home. But after ten minutes she went to sleep with the set still on.

She was awakened by the sound of Paul's key in the lock. "Where are you?" he called out irritably. "I knocked and knocked."

Fuzzy with sleep, she sat up in bed. "I'm sorry." At the sight of him, tall and gaunt in the doorway, his hair disheveled and his face un-smiling, her own smile died on her lips. Evident-ly he was still going to carry on the quarrel they'd had this morning.

"Are you this exhausted from that damned job?" he snapped. Turning, he walked away. She heard him in the kitchen, slamming the refrig-erator door. "There's nothing here to eat!" he yelled.

She lay very still on the bed, not answering.

She heard him coming back to the bedroom. "I said, is that job making you this tired?"

"No, the *job* isn't," she said with sudden bit-terness. "But the cooking and laundry and mop-ping and sweeping and . . . other things are."

He still stood in the doorway, glaring at her. "Maybe you need a vacation from being mar-ried."

"Maybe I do. And maybe I'll take it next week."

He came into the room, glaring at her. "What does that mean?"

"It means I may go to Boston and Philadelphia with Erica. She's going on a business trip." She hadn't meant to say it so suddenly; it had just slipped out. Now she wanted to go, very much— to stay in a fine hotel, to be waited on, for a change, to be in the midst of excitement, if only for a little while.

"Well, isn't that great?" he sneered. "You never said anything about traveling on this job. I suppose the Ice Princess insisted."

"No, she didn't." Jenny told him exactly what Erica had said.

"Well, that's even worse," he raged. "You *want* to go."

"Yes. I *do*. And I will." He stormed out of the apartment and Jenny was too tired to wait up for his return. As she drifted off to sleep she thought, I'll call Erica tomorrow and tell her I'm going.

Chapter Four

Erica slept until noon the next day, Saturday, and woke refreshed and full of her old confidence. Her Aunt Merry was out, so she breakfasted in peaceful solitude in the sunny dining room, enjoying the sight of the bright-blue September sky above the trim brownstones across the way.

She bathed slowly and dressed casually in a lightweight crocheted sweater the color of cream and pants of cream, russet and forest-green houndstooth check. She put on russet boots and, because the day was so mild, a cream cardigan. She left her shining hair free. Taking her portfolio, she slung a russet bag over her shoulder and ran down the back stairs to the garage.

She drove downtown with a feeling of optimism and elation. A couple of times she idly noted a powerful black Jaguar in her rearview mirror, but gave it no particular thought.

She loved the quiet granite canyons of Wall Street on weekends; the narrow streets were comparatively deserted—an austere etching of tall shadows and fluttering pigeons. This afternoon the hardy urban birds almost covered the statue of Washington in front of the Stock Exchange. Erica parked quite near the Warren Building.

When she was locking her car she saw the big black Jag drawing up in the space behind her. It stopped and Steven Kimball got out. Erica started to move away, but he called out, "Erica, wait."

He came striding toward her and she had a peculiar sensation of invaded privacy. There seemed to be no escape from this exasperating man; somehow she always thought of Wall Street on Saturdays as hers, a place where she rarely ran into anyone she knew. And here was Steven Kimball again.

But as he reached her Erica was even more disturbed to feel a quick flutter in her pulse, a warmth in her body. She told herself that she disliked him intensely, yet at this moment he looked very appealing. His powerful body was frankly outlined by his tight-fitting clothes—a casual but obviously expensive gray knit shirt with red stripes, open at the neck; snug gray denim trousers and mahogany boots.

The colors made the thick black hair springing up in a vital thatch from his proud head look inky, and enhanced the bronzed tone of his skin. Against that tan those piercing silver eyes were more striking than ever; his likeness to a pirate was pronounced.

Damn him, she thought. Why did someone she hated have to look like that? Very deliberately she composed her expression.

"So," he said, in that deep, growling voice, "we've discovered each other's dark secret."

"And what would that be, Mr. Kimball?" She stared up into his eyes, determined not to let him see how much he upset her. Her voice was cool and calm, a little amused.

"That all work makes Jack and Jill a dull couple and closet compulsives," he commented, grinning.

"You may be Jack, but I'm no one's Jill," she retorted. "Now, if you'll excuse me, I have to get to my office." Erica turned away to avoid the disturbing sight of his dazzling smile in that dark face.

"'Have to'?" he teased. "Why, Erica, is there some divine timekeeper standing there with a celestial watch, threatening your immortal soul?"

His tone infuriated her. He spoke as if she were a little girl intent on making mud pies. "In the first place, it's none of your business. In the second place, what are *you* doing here? You must have some kind of timekeeper yourself."

"I have to drop in at my office for a while," he admitted. "But actually I was following you."

"Still trying to find a place for lunch?" she countered. "If that's the case you must be faint from hunger." Again she made a move as if to walk away.

"I'm never faint from anything, Erica. Wait a minute." He reached out and touched her arm and she was even more annoyed that the touch sent a little shiver along her nerves. She moved her arm away abruptly. "Come on, Erica," he said in a cajoling tone.

Then he raised his strong arms in a gesture of surrender. "I give up. Your tongue's too sharp even for me. But now that you mention it, how *about* lunch?"

"I just had breakfast." She moved off in the direction of the Warren Building.

"Well, then, let's walk a little. I have to pass your place to get to mine."

"I can't prevent you," she said stiffly and he fell into step beside her, shortening his long stride to match hers.

"This is a great place on off-days, isn't it?"

The sudden switch of mood, the softness and confidentiality of his tone, threw her completely off.

She found herself answering with simple openness. "I love it. I used to come here with my grandfather a lot on Saturdays and Sundays when he was alive." Erica was dismayed to hear the trembling in her voice.

Steven Kimball touched her shoulder with a friendly gesture. "You've been a very lonely lady, haven't you, Erica?"

She stiffened. She had let this manipulator see too much of her real self and suddenly she resented it. "Why on earth do you say that?" she asked coolly.

"Because it's true."

Reluctantly she glanced up at him for a moment; he was looking down at her, smiling. But tender as his words had sounded, the smile was not tender. It was triumphant, self-satisfied and smug. He had the expression of a man who liked taking people apart, analyzing the parts and enjoying the rightness of his diagnosis. Well, he's not going to psychoanalyze *me*, she concluded.

"Will I get a bill from you, Doctor, or is this a free consultation?"

Something flickered in the depths of his silver-gray eyes but she couldn't quite tell whether it was anger, disappointment or triumph. What a puzzle the man was.

He ignored the taunt and asked, "How long do you think you'll be?"

They were standing in front of the Warren Building now and Erica noticed that the guard was studying them with great interest. She was friendly with the guard, who was used to her coming in on weekends, but somehow today she disliked being the object of his interest.

"I really have no idea," she answered in freezing tones. "Now if you'll excuse me—"

"I'll call you at home late this afternoon," Kimball said.

His arrogant disregard of her unwillingness to have anything to do with him stung Erica into another sharp answer. "I really don't know why. Don't waste your time."

Erica walked away from him and past the surprised guard—she usually had a friendly word for the man—and jabbed at the button of the private elevator. She heard Kimball's amused laughter through the open door and it made her angrier than ever.

Her mind was still on the unwelcome encounter when she entered the unlocked office and heard the clatter of a typewriter from Jenny's area. Her assistant, dressed in a soft yellow sweater and jeans, was busily typing at her desk.

Erica was still off balance. The meeting with Steven Kimball hadn't lasted more than five or ten minutes at the most and yet it seemed she'd been with him for hours. The strangeness of it was unsettling. She really needed a private moment to sort it all out and was hard put to greet Jenny with any degree of poise.

Jenny looked up and smiled. "Well, hello again. I called you at home, but you'd already left."

Erica pulled herself together and smiled back. "How nice! This must mean you're going on the trip." She rested her portfolio on Jenny's desk to disguise the trembling of her hands.

"Yes. I've already phoned Shirlee. I remembered that the memo, with all the details, was here, so I had to come in anyway. I *thought* you'd be coming in." Erica had the sudden feeling that Jenny's cheerfulness was as forced as her own calm. The girl's smile wavered; she was chattering the way she always did when she was nervous or uncertain. "You look great," she said to Erica.

"So do you. But you seem a little . . . tired," Erica replied carefully. Jenny's nose was pink and her eyes were swollen. "How are things on the home front?"

"Don't ask."

"I'll ask later, if you'll let me. What time do you have to be home?"

"No special time," Jenny said. "Paul's working and he won't be home until at least seven."

"Good." Erica picked up her portfolio, relieved that her hands were steadier. "I have to put in a couple of hours. I want to get things squared away for the other secretaries. Maybe we can have a late lunch . . . or early dinner, whichever it is." She grinned. "All right?"

She thought: It's a perfect way to avoid *his* call, too.

"I'd love it," Jenny said warmly. She looked brighter. "I've done some squaring away, too. It's on your desk."

"You're the best." Erica went on into her office and sat down at her desk. Checking the memoranda Jenny had put there she thought: Squared away isn't the word. I've got almost nothing left to do.

She had other matters to see to, however, and the encounter with Steven Kimball wasn't helping her concentration. But she turned to the business at hand, dictating six long memos into a tape recorder and putting the tape into Jenny's basket to pass along to the others. Then she tackled the problem uppermost in her mind—the acquisition of Warren stock by the Kimren Corporation. She had been too preoccupied yesterday to pursue it, but now she was determined to get to the bottom of it. She was tempted to postpone the Boston trip for another day so she could start her detective work on Monday, when the Exchange was open.

But that would be too great an inconvenience to everybody. And there were still several phone calls she could make today, Saturday or not, to knowledgeable sources. She got out her private list of phone numbers and began to make the calls. Four of the people were away for the weekend; the fifth was as much in the dark as she.

Making a sound of exasperation, she gave it up for the moment and went to the bookshelves lining the wall by her desk. After finding the volume she was seeking she took it back to her desk and began to study the vast, tangled network of Kimco enterprises, trying to find a clue. She could find none.

She replaced the book and took out another, studying the corporate structure of Warren. Erica smiled wryly; compared to Kimco, Warren's setup was as uncomplicated as a child's pile of building blocks. She sighed, thinking, I'm just spinning my wheels. She'd gone through this before in her fascinated studies of Kimco. How the man did it she still wasn't quite sure and she felt an unwilling admiration war with her resentment against Steven Kimball. He's got more twists than a pretzel, she reflected; she'd be willing to bet he was the only one, in the last analysis, who could untangle the mystery of Kimco. And how wise that was. It made other corporate entities sitting ducks for a takeover and left him totally secure.

A light tap on the door startled her. Jenny was standing in the doorway. "Excuse me. Do you know what time it is?"

"No, as a matter of fact." Erica put down the book.

"Four o'clock."

"It *can't* be!" Erica exclaimed, but a glance at her gold watch told her that it was. "Unbelievable." She laughed. "I didn't realize; I was really out of it there." She got up and replaced the book; then she slipped her empty portfolio into a bottom drawer of her desk.

"Well," she said brightly, "how about you? Are you all done?"

"All done."

"Shall we, then?" Erica got up from her chair.

"We shall," Jenny answered cheerfully. "I'll just put these tapes away and then we can take off."

They didn't speak during the quick descent to

street level. Erica wished the guard a nice Sunday, saying to Jenny as they came into the mild air, "I'm parked right over there." The black Jaguar, she noticed, was gone.

When they were settled in the Mercedes Jenny leaned back against the leather seats with an exaggerated groan of pleasure, commenting, "This sure does beat the IRT."

Erica laughed. "It sure does." She had a fleeting picture of the relative difficulty and limitations of Jenny's life, thinking, I'd like to do more for her. And with surprise Erica realized that Jenny was probably the best friend she had in the world, the only one who really understood her.

"Where shall we eat?" she asked Jenny. "How about someplace in your neighborhood? That'll be convenient for you."

"Oh, wonderful." Jenny sighed. She sounded so delighted that Erica felt for a moment as if she were taking a child out for a treat.

Erica drove easily uptown, twisting and turning among the winding Village streets until they reached their destination. Happily there was a parking place quite near the restaurant they had chosen.

After they were settled in a secluded booth and had ordered, Erica asked quietly, "Now, what is all this about at home? Tell me about it, would you?"

Relaxed and confiding, Jenny began to talk to Erica as she never had before. Hesitant at first, she soon became totally open, admitting to small resentments that had obviously bothered her for a long time. At first, she said, everything had been utterly idyllic with her and Paul, but lately he had shown an increasing hostility toward her aims and ideas.

"He's always saying I've 'joined the Establishment,'" Jenny remarked bitterly. "Even wanting to cut my hair is a sign of being cold and career oriented."

"Oh, honestly," Erica put down her glass with such indignant force that some of her sherry splashed out on the old wooden table. "You do have gorgeous hair and I know how men are about long hair. But you could be utterly feminine with a nice cut, maybe just to the collar. I've often pictured that."

"I know." Jenny sighed. She went on to describe her other grievances and problems. Erica got a picture of a confused and angry young man who seemed totally self-involved. Jenny told her that he had already turned down two very good job offers and would soon graduate—with nowhere to go.

"I think he's a frustrated Frank Lloyd Wright," Jenny commented after a pause while the waitress placed their dishes before them. She attacked her steak with great appetite; apparently her confession had relaxed her.

Marriage, Erica thought as she began eating her own lunch, is not always what it's cracked up to be. It wasn't the first time she'd heard things like this and she suddenly was delighted with her own freedom.

As Jenny went on talking Erica learned that they had quarreled the night before and had hardly been speaking this morning when Paul left for work.

"Well," Erica said tactfully after dessert was brought, "I hope things are better tonight. And that you'll have a nice day tomorrow. You're sure you still want to come with me?"

"Very sure. The first three stops will only take four or five days and I think maybe it'll do him good to be on his own. Maybe he'll appreciate how much I do when I'm not there to do it." Jenny smiled a little crookedly and Erica couldn't help having reservations.

However, all she said was, "Well, it'll be wonderful to have your company. I think that's what I want more than anything . . . your company and encouragement. Secretarial service I can get anywhere." She grinned at the blond girl.

"So"—Erica took out one of her credit cards and paid the bill—"we'll meet Monday morning. One of our drivers will take us to the airport. Why don't I have him pick you up at your house at about eight-thirty? Then he'll pick me up and drive us to JFK."

"It sounds heavenly."

They walked out of the quiet restaurant onto the tree-lined but crowded street.

"I guess if I drove you home," Erica said humorously, "it would take three hours."

"It would. I can walk the three blocks before you get to Eighth Avenue." Jenny laughed, then sobered. "Thank you, Erica. Thank you so much . . . for the wonderful lunch . . . for asking me on the trip. For everything."

"You're the one to thank, Jenny." Erica kept

her voice light, but she felt a deep gratitude and affection for the loyal girl. "See you Monday. Have a nice evening."

She watched Jenny walk east with slow, rather hesitant steps; then she went to the car. The Saturday-evening traffic was getting thick and the drive uptown was slow and exasperating, but Erica was feeling very fortunate indeed.

It occurred to her that if she kept cool enough the war with Steven Kimball could still be won. She might even enjoy the battle.

When she got home she found a note on the hall table indicating that a Mr. Kimball had phoned twice, at 4:00 and 5:30 P.M. But now the thought of him didn't affect her at all; she was still feeling too good about being unattached and not under some man's thumb, the way poor Jenny was.

Erica's feeling of freedom and renewed vitality carried her through a pleasant evening. She went to a concert and had a late supper with friends, delighted to be on her own in a group for a change and not saddled with Morgan. She couldn't imagine what had possessed her to keep on dating him.

She slept very late again the next morning and when she woke knew that her reserves of energy were fully replenished. She was eager for the day and night to pass; she couldn't wait to get on the plane tomorrow.

Merry had gone to church and, Erica supposed, was lunching with someone.

She spent some time packing, a chore she

rarely left to others because she enjoyed it so much herself. Thanks to super-efficient Jenny's advance forecasts Erica was able to plan exactly what to pack on top. On the bottom she packed the lighter clothes she would need in Miami and the Southwest. The Midwest and Coast, she knew, would be utterly unpredictable, but most likely her mid-weight ensembles would serve. And, this way, with the chore done, she was free for the evening—if she wanted to be. She had been invited to a museum benefit, but she wasn't sure whether she felt like going or not.

At dinner that night she told her aunt enthusiastically about the trip, omitting for the moment to mention the matter of the mysterious Kimren stock purchase. There was no point in worrying Merry until she had more information. After all, she only had George's word that Kimren *was* Steven Kimball, and George, Erica reflected darkly, was about as stable as a wind chime in a hurricane.

"You're looking very chipper," Merry said approvingly. "I really don't know what to make of you, child. I really thought you were working too hard, but apparently it agrees with you. Evidently opposition brings out the best in you, the way it always did in Josh." Erica had told her about the board's hostility toward the Erin Division and the amazing loan from Merchants Andover. "But," she added, "you do neglect your social life, my dear."

Erica protested that she'd been out the night before. "Besides, when this trip is over"—and, she added mentally, when I've settled the matter of those blasted stocks—"I might take a little time off."

"It's always when such-and-such is over," Merry commented in a dry voice. "Don't let your youth fly by without some fun, Erica. I did and now I regret it greatly. Of course," she continued with a smile, "I'm making up for it now in my wild middle age."

"You'll be playing bridge with the sharks tonight, I take it." Erica's tone was flippant but affectionate.

"But of course. And I'll have a grand time showing off my new Rogue." She held up her graceful hands to the lapels of her blue-gray prototype ensemble, one of the more conservative and higher-priced designs of which Erica was particularly proud. "I brag about my niece everywhere. I really don't know how you've done it, darling. These clothes are delightful. It's fun to advertise for you. But are you *sure* this isn't too young? I don't want to look like mutton dressed as lamb."

"What utter nonsense," Erica protested.

Merry went happily off to her engagement and for a moment Erica was a little at a loss. She felt too wide-awake to stay in; perhaps, she decided, she'd go to the museum benefit after all. She had been planning to avoid it because the same old crowd would be on hand. She didn't want to run into Morgan, or George and Arabella, who went to absolutely everything.

But it was such a mild, lovely evening. And she'd have an excuse to wear a new dress she hadn't worn yet. The idea was appealing. Erica went upstairs and showered again, making up with care. Then she slipped into the dress; it was a delight—a short, chocolate-brown taffeta with a deep ruffled hem and extravagant sleeves that reminded her of giant, crisp flower petals. She wore no jewels at all. Her dark-brown patterned stockings and coffee-colored suede sandals, barely more than a strap and a needle-thin heel, made her legs look sensational.

She pulled her hair back, wanting it to be very plain to compensate for the flirty shortness and froufrou ruffles of the dress, which did amazing things for her dark brown eyes and richly colored hair. She looked at herself in the full-length mirror and smiled. Merry was right; Josh had been right, too. She was a woman, after all, and it was great fun to be reminded of that fact occasionally.

Erica put a few essentials into a small leather bag and decided not to bother with a coat at all. The air was positively summery, as often happened in the city at this time of year, and she planned to come right home after the benefit, anyway, so she could get up very early in the morning.

She hummed to herself as she drove to Fifth Avenue. She parked on a side street and walked around the corner to the Frick Museum, a block-long converted mansion, a sculptured masterpiece of limestone built in 1913 by a famous and tough manufacturer for his residence. Every cornice, balustrade and wrought-iron fence was carefully designed to harmonize, and the building housed an exquisite and noted collection.

Erica went into the imposing gallery in which the benefit was being held, hearing the ripple of Bach from the great pipe organ on the landing of the grand marble staircase. She saw several people she knew and spoke to them casually, waving to others. Her glance rested momentarily on one of her favorite paintings, a Rembrandt self-portrait.

Without enthusiasm she returned the greeting of Arabella Loving, as usual scantily dressed in a barely-there confection of magenta that was mostly straps on top. Erica's cousin George was leaning against the wall next to Arabella; he seemed drunk.

"Erica." She recognized Morgan's correct voice and turned to greet him in a cool, calm fashion. "My dear," he said, "you look stunning. But I'm surprised to see you. When I asked you to come here you told me you'd be busy." He smiled ruefully and she felt the familiar irritation with his persistence and his somewhat martyred manner.

"I thought I would be," she said crisply, "but, as it turned out, I wasn't." This is ridiculous, she thought. Why do I owe him an explanation?

"Can I get you something?" he asked solicitously.

"All right . . . thanks," she said grudgingly. "A sherry."

"At once. Don't go away." With a smile he hurried off to the bar.

Erica looked around the room; there was quite a crowd milling about under the rare paintings by Goya and Velázquez, El Greco and Renoir,

Turner and Whistler and Gainsborough, their feet soundless on the ancient Persian carpets, their chatter loud and constant.

Under one of the Goya paintings she glimpsed two men and her absent gaze began to sweep past them. One of the men looked like every man she knew, but his companion was exceedingly striking and tall. His dark, thick hair was as night-black as that of the Spanish grandee in the Goya painting and his skin was tanned almost mahogany. Erica looked at him more closely; as the group in front of him moved away she was able to see him quite clearly. It was Steven Kimball. He turned his head and saw her; in his dark face those unique silver eyes seemed to burn.

Erica quickly looked away and walked toward a Renoir painting, pretending to study it with great attention. Yet she couldn't resist watching Kimball out of the corner of her eye. He was coming toward her. She felt an adrenaline born of anger and excitement pumping in her veins.

At that moment Morgan returned with her wine. He almost collided with Steven Kimball.

"I beg your pardon," Kimball said in his rough voice, with an extravagant bow of apology. He was still the same mocking devil he'd always been, Erica thought, smiling her thanks at Morgan as she took the small sherry glass from his fingers.

"Miss Warren, Mr. Hunt," Steven said formally.

"Mr. Kimball," she answered coldly. With perfect deliberation she took a sip of her wine and walked away to look up at a picture by Ingres. Morgan followed. Kimball stood where he was and when she glanced at him again he was studying her with a mocking look.

"Erica," Morgan said in a low voice, "there's something we must talk about."

She was totally exasperated. Standing, as she was, in full view of Steven Kimball, she couldn't humiliate Morgan by walking away. On the other hand, it annoyed her to have Kimball witness this scene; he was most likely guessing what it was about. "We've talked about it," she whispered, keeping her expression blank. "No."

"It's not that," he insisted in the same low tone. "It's about the stocks."

She felt her interest quicken, but before she could say anything Arabella's sharp, affected voice broke in. "Well, here's an interesting group of marbles." Erica wondered what she was leading up to; there were no statues near them. She soon found out.

"Warren, Hunt and Kimball, that is," Arabella went on, her words carrying clearly. "This bunch belongs on a pedestal together." People were starting to stare. George was standing with his arm around Arabella's waist, as if propping her up. "Be very careful, Georgie, not to brush against them. Uptightness is infectious; we'll catch it."

Erica looked at Kimball; his face was pitying, a little disgusted. Under her embarrassment Erica was elated. It was obvious that they were

not together, that something had happened between them to anger Arabella into making this
public display. Something, she reflected, or
nothing. That was it. Nothing had happened
between them. Was it possible? Erica was irrationally delighted; it put Steven Kimball in a
whole new light.

"Take it easy, Bella." George was pulling at
her as if to urge her away. Morgan glared at
George. More heads were turning; others stared
in frank enjoyment at the scene, which would
very likely make the next day's gossip columns.

Erica walked calmly away, moving down the
gallery as if nothing at all had happened, studying other paintings in a leisurely fashion. Whatever the others did, she thought, she was going
to get away. She did not look back.

She set her half-empty sherry glass on the bar
and walked out into the garden, taking a relieved breath of the cooling air. It was almost
dark; the evening had that wonderful dark-blue
color that sometimes reminded her of Paris and
the trees were friendly masses of whispering
darkness where the light breeze stirred their
limbs. Then she heard a firm footstep on the
flagstones behind her.

"Miss Warren." Her heart leaped; she knew
that rough, rather angry voice, whose tones
affected her like stroking hands. "Don't run
away the way you did from Miller's," the voice
commanded. She still hadn't turned around.
"You're as hard to pin down in person as you are
on the phone."

Well, she wouldn't run this time, she vowed. She wouldn't give him the satisfaction. And it would be quite interesting to see what he might give away about Kimren.

She turned around then and looked at him. In the soft, dim light of the evening he stared back at her, his dark face brooding, unreadable. He looked bigger than ever in a tan sport jacket that emphasized the breadth of his shoulders.

Against the pale tan of the jacket his skin looked more deeply tanned than ever; his hair had that startling blackness and, as always, the silver eyes gleamed at her in the twilight with the brightness of illuminated water. They reminded Erica of moonlight on the sea.

A chill of excitement ran along her flesh, but she was determined to give him no hint of the effect he had on her. "Bored with the pictures, Mr. Kimball?" She was delighted with her own coolness.

"*Those* pictures, yes. Although this isn't the best light for viewing." He took a step toward her, looking her up and down with open admiration. There was no mockery in his look and she felt her heartbeat accelerate, her breathing quicken. This was not going to be as easy as she had anticipated.

She couldn't find the flippant reply she so desperately wanted. But she sensed that he was at a loss for words now himself and somehow that gave her a great feeling of satisfaction.

To cover her confusion she looked up at the sky and said conversationally, "It's a lovely night."

"A very lovely night." His voice was softer than she had ever heard it. "Shall we walk a little?"

She nodded and he joined her on the flagstone path, where they strolled along. He was so close beside her that his arm brushed hers, and a quick, dismaying heat flared up her arm to her shoulder. She heard the rushing of her own excited blood and the flutter of her pulses in her ears, louder than their steps on the stones.

"I must be going soon," she said abruptly.

"So early?" The growl of his voice vibrated within her as his arm touched hers again.

"I'm leaving town early tomorrow on business."

"So am I," he answered. "I've been on a . . . kind of holiday, but I've got to get back to work." She glanced up at him then; he was smiling down at her and she was more than ever disconcerted by his extraordinary magnetism. Those strange silver eyes bore into hers.

Quickly she looked away, keeping her gaze straight ahead. "Surely you've already gone back to work," she retorted.

"How so?"

"On the Exchange." She glanced up at him again to see if the shot had hit home.

But to her annoyance his face was utterly blank and he merely smiled a lopsided smile. "Not really. I assign a lot of my dirty work to others. That's something I'd like to teach you, Miss Warren. In fact"—he slowed his steps and stopped—"there's more than one thing I'd like to teach you."

Before she knew what had happened he had grabbed her in his arms. Then, with one steely hand holding her to his body, he cupped her face roughly with the other and turned it up to his. Slowly, deliberately he brought his face down to hers. She was still, but a deep trembling began inside her.

I'm hypnotized, she thought, amazed. I simply cannot move. He knew it, too, and the knowledge brought a triumphant smile to his insolent mouth, the mouth that was drawing nearer and nearer, with half-parted lips, to her own.

She came to her senses and began to struggle in his grasp. But now the relentless mouth was on hers and she couldn't control the sound of ecstatic pleasure that escaped her, couldn't withstand his nearness and the fiery excitement of that kiss. She relaxed utterly, melting softly and bonelessly against his hard body.

Finally he released her for a moment from the dizzying kiss, drawing his dark head backward a little to look down into her face, and she could see his amazement, his delight.

"I knew this; I knew it," he whispered hoarsely and then he was kissing her again and again she was helpless under his touch, dimly wondering what it was he'd known; but all thought ceased under the demanding caress of his mouth and she could only feel, feel a sweet astonishment as her body answered him in a way she had never known, a wild and hungry way no other man had ever shown her in her life.

Now she was not only submitting—she was responding with a savage yearning so alien to her that she felt her very self dissolve; she moved closer, reached up with her trembling hands to his head, stroking his thick, vital hair. Her fingers wandered downward from his head to touch his ears and then the beating hollows below them; his pulse felt like a pounding drum. He made a sound that was almost a groan of pain and she knew he was deeply shaken. His body shuddered under her lightest touch; he took his lips from her mouth, and, quivering with anticipation that was a kind of dread, she felt the firm lips lightly kiss her cheek, moving swiftly to the side of her neck, then downward to her throat, all the while feeling his hard hands explore her, her bare arms, the narrow expanse of her waist where it swelled into her slender hips, rising again to learn the shape of her pulsating breasts.

He raised his head and spoke in a low, shaken voice. "This is what I knew, Erica, from the first moment I ever touched you."

She had surrendered so completely to his embrace that at first she hardly realized how little tenderness there was in the words. Then, bitterly, she understood the hardness in him; it was the sound of triumph and gratification. Steven Kimball was a gamesman, she thought, a gamesman in the art of conquest, and now his curiosity had been satisfied.

"I knew; I knew," he said, "that you couldn't be cold to me." He smiled.

His smile confirmed the thing she feared: She had been a challenge to him simply because she had the reputation of being cold. But now that he had proven all the others wrong he was gloating at her. How could she have let this happen? How could she have let it get this far? To him she was merely a romantic conquest, his victim in a financial coup. And she'd reacted like a teen-ager overwhelmed by her first kiss.

"If your mission's accomplished, let me go." He was so taken aback that he let go of her at once, taking a backward step and staring down at her, nonplussed. She had spoken as coldly as she knew how and was glad to see him rattled.

"My mission?" he repeated blankly.

"I know your plans for Warren, Mr. Kimball. I haven't tracked down Kimren yet, but I'll get to that, I'm sure. But *this* takeover stops here."

He was still staring. She couldn't quite read the sharp, sudden brightness in those silver eyes. How wrong people were, it came to her then, to say that dark eyes were mysterious. Kimball's eyes blinded her by their very brightness to what was behind them.

"Stops with a kiss?" he asked, amused. "You're a gorgeous woman, but you sound like a nineteenth-century novel."

Hot with anger, she retorted, "I don't like being mauled."

"You loved it," he countered. "And you were hardly being 'mauled,' in any case. As for this . . . Kimren, was it? . . . It's news to me. It's probably a rip-off off the Kimco name. That happens every day. It happened to *you* when 'Erren' tried to rip off Erin."

He seemed almost relieved to move from personal topics to business.

But she was still unconvinced. "You recalled the name very well, Mr. Kimball. And you know quite a lot about Warren. Anyway, why bother to justify yourself if you're innocent?"

He frowned and his lips tightened. "You missed your calling, Miss Warren. You would have made a great prosecuting attorney . . . in the days of Cotton Mather, with your puritan hang-ups."

Kimball studied her face and she knew he could see her hurt and indignation. He smiled his lopsided smile and tugged at a thick lock of his black hair.

"I ask your forgiveness, my lady, for the liberties I took with you. You won't be telling the master, will you, and get me fired from the stables?" he asked in a parody of an uneasy servant.

Erica was so humiliated by his teasing that she could find no reply. He obviously thought she was a silly fool, a kind of dinosaur, with her rigid ideas about behavior.

"Good night, Miss Warren," he said blandly. Turning on his heel, he went back into the building.

Erica saw his tall, strong body outlined against the light that streamed into the dark from the gallery, his proud head held high as he strode away from her like a conqueror from a field of battle. She saw someone join him at the door, saw the man's mouth form an unheard question. Steven Kimball nodded his head and laughed.

She was stung; perhaps they'd even made a

bet about her, the way college boys did. She was determined to forget him once and for all except as a financial antagonist. That battle wasn't finished by a long shot.

She walked directly to Fifth Avenue. As she walked to her car she knew with a sinking feeling she would never be able to get Kimball out of her mind.

His kiss was still on her mouth; her skin tingled with the remembered touch of his hard, strong hands; her very body recalled the form of him. He would be with her, like a taunting ghost, on the plane tomorrow, on all the planes she would take in the weeks that followed; to the north and east, the south and west, the memory of his closeness would go, too.

Chapter Five

The next morning Erica was doubly glad she had asked Jenny to come along on the trip to Boston. She herself had been to Boston many times, but Jenny, who had traveled so seldom, was thrilled with everything and Erica was able to enjoy her enjoyment, distracting herself from the unsettling encounter the night before.

Erica gave Jenny the window seat on the plane; she herself lay back with half-closed eyes during the brief flight, tired from a restless night. As it had done last night, the thought of Steven Kimball kept intruding. After a while she gave up the idea of a nap and opened her portfolio, taking out her Boston notes. She was soon immersed in them, all her attention on the day ahead.

After they touched down at Logan and disembarked, Erica guided Jenny through the terminal to the spot where the Warren driver would pick them up.

The driver was waiting for them and Erica greeted him warmly. "It's really good to see you, Harry. I'm glad they sent you." Harry had been one of Josh's favorite drivers. Erica introduced him to Jenny and he quickly stowed their luggage away. In moments they had begun the three-mile drive to the city.

The day was crisp and clear and Erica continued to enjoy Jenny's excitement. "Later on we'll take a look at the city from the Prudential Skywalk or the Hancock Tower," Erica promised her with a smile.

It seemed no time at all before Harry deposited them before the Copley Plaza, Boston's sister hotel to New York's famed Plaza. As he handed over their luggage to the hotel attendants he asked Erica, "Will you be needing me in town, Miss Warren?"

"No, thanks, Harry." Erica gave him an affectionate pat on the shoulder. "Mrs. Landon hasn't seen Boston before and we'll be doing a lot of walking. I can call a cab for anything else."

He wished her a good stay and drove off. When they entered the elegant Copley, Jenny stepped with delighted awe onto the mosaic floors, glancing at the rich wood paneling and gilded ceilings. Chandeliers of Waterford crystal and antique furniture graced the lobby.

After they were in their suite Jenny looked around. "I can't believe it," she said. "A fireplace and an antique china cabinet!"

"It's a marvelous place," Erica agreed. "Let's check out the bedrooms. I have a feeling that by tonight I'm going to be yearning for my bed."

Their rooms featured quilted floral bedspreads, plush velvet chairs, thick rugs and marble-topped night tables.

Erica wandered in her stocking feet back into the sitting room. "Would you like some coffee?" she called.

"*Love* some. Shall I order?"

"I'll do it." Erica phoned for room service. As she did so she glanced idly at a New York tabloid she had picked up in the lobby, along with several other papers. The blaring headline rang a bell but, as she spoke into the phone, it didn't quite register.

But when her call was completed she looked at it again. MR. MASK UNMASKED, it said. Below was the clearest picture she had ever seen of Steven Kimball. He was leaving the museum with three chic women around him and there was a fearsome frown on his pirate face.

Erica grinned maliciously; how he must have hated that.

Jenny came back; she had changed from her green Erin ensemble into a wool skirt and blazer. "I think it's a bit chilly out there," she remarked.

Erica agreed. "I think I'll put on something

warmer, too. Just sign when the coffee comes," she added and went into her own room. She had already unpacked what she'd need in Boston and now hung the clothes quickly in the large closet.

She took off her suit and hung it, too, choosing a skirt in tawny autumn plaids, a soft sweater-blouse of bronzed green and a short trim jacket in camel that harmonized with the plaid. She slipped on medium-heeled shoes of tan leather which matched the shoulder bag she'd carried on the plane.

When she returned to the living room she tossed her portfolio onto a chair, along with her jacket. The coffee had arrived. Erica sat down beside Jenny on the couch and took her first grateful sip.

It annoyed her that the picture of Steven Kimball was still vivid in her mind, although she had turned the tabloid face-down to get it out of sight. Three women, no less, she thought. But there would always be women around him—even if he didn't have a penny. She shivered suddenly, feeling a peculiar chill. The memory of his kiss, his touch, was still too recent.

"Are you all right?" Jenny asked anxiously.

"Oh, fine," she answered casually, "just a little sleepy. But we're going to have a very busy day. Are you up to it?"

"Absolutely."

"Well, enjoy your coffee. I'm going to glance at the papers and I have some calls to make, now that it's late enough. Unfinished business from Friday." She smiled.

Tactfully sensing that Erica might want to be alone, Jenny said, "You know, I could use a second breakfast. I just realized I'm starving. Is there anything like a coffee shop in this castle?"

"More or less. Go ahead; I'll find you."

When Jenny had gone Erica eagerly scanned the *Wall Street Journal* and the financial sections of the other papers. Nothing, no clue. She went to the phone and put through calls to her New York contacts, then to the Warren attorneys. Still nothing. They said they'd "get to work on it right away." After that she even tried some Boston prospects, with the same result.

She found Jenny in the lobby, staring at the famous works of art on the walls, the splendor that had attracted so many celebrities to the Copley over the years.

They walked briskly out into the bright-blue autumn day and took a taxi to the Prudential Skywalk so Jenny could get a view of Boston from the enclosed observation deck. Once there, a 360-degree panorama of the famous old city spread out before them. They could see for miles, as far as the mountains of southern New Hampshire. Jenny took a look at Cape Cod through one of the coin-fed telescopes.

She was able to get the general layout of Boston below: Boston's famous wharves; the Bunker Hill Monument; the dock where "Old Ironsides" was anchored. In the center was the long green stretch of Boston Common. To the right of Commonwealth Avenue she saw the famous Charles River that separated Boston from Cambridge and, farther on, Back Bay.

"Well, young lady," Erica said, glancing at her watch, "let's get to work."

As Erica had promised Jenny, they had a very busy day, visiting Erin Hideouts at several major stores.

After a quick lunch they visited real estate agents, who came up with several prospective locations for the boutique which they would be shown the next morning.

"It's gone so well," Erica said, "that we can just goof off tomorrow afternoon and leave for Philly Wednesday morning. I'll only need one day there, so it'll be Washington Thursday. You can get back to New York by Friday, at the latest. That should please Paul."

Jenny didn't return her smile. "I hope so."

"What's all this?" When Jenny hesitated Erica said, "You know, it's past time for dinner. I think it's also time we talked again. And then, for me, a very early night. I'm tired."

"So am I," Jenny admitted. "I didn't sleep much last night."

"I didn't, either. Too much sleep the nights before," Erica said lightly, thinking: What a liar I am. We both lost sleep over men—Jenny over a man she knows too well, me over one I don't know at all. "How about dinner at the hotel? Their restaurants are marvelous. Then we can just go upstairs and collapse."

"That's a great idea."

Copley's Bar and Restaurant was an eating place with one name but several faces; besides the barroom and the lounge, with its stained-glass fixtures and plants, there were three small dining rooms. Jenny and Erica dined in one of these, which, with its Edwardian decor, was reminiscent of an English club.

Jenny experimented with Bombay-style curry and Erica savored a prime filet stuffed with peppers, onions and mushrooms. They discussed business until dessert, skirting around Jenny's problem. But when they were being served coffee and liqueurs Erica said gently, "Tell me about the weekend."

Jenny did, saying that things were worse at home. They had quarreled again Saturday night and Paul had stormed off to his parents' house in upper New York State. He hadn't come back by Sunday night. She assumed he had gotten back in time for his classes Monday.

"Call him tonight, Jenny," Erica urged her.

"He knows where to reach me," Jenny said stubbornly. "I left him my itinerary."

Erica didn't reply, thinking: Who am I to advise her? She couldn't even handle being kissed. The thought was absurd, humiliating, and it haunted her all the way up in the elevator.

"Early as it is," she said in the suite, "I'm calling it a night."

"Me, too." Jenny smiled a little uncertainly. Subdued, they went to their rooms.

Erica took a long bath and went to bed with a book. In a very short time, despite her disturbed thoughts and her many plans for the next morning, she was overcome by sleep.

The weather on Tuesday was a repetition of the day before: wonderful autumn weather, but a little milder. They made short work of finding a boutique location; Erica was immediately taken by a vacancy in the Quincy Market's northern sector. The North Market, which catered to the younger set, was just the place for a shop to be called, simply, Hideout, stocking the low-priced Steal line.

Elated, Erica returned to the agent's office with Jenny and signed a lease. Her next step was an appointment with a local woman executive who was brilliant with personnel and marketing. She had a hundred things to discuss, among them the recruitment of local talent to staff the Quincy Market Hideout and the advisability of some personnel changes in two of the department-store Hideouts.

Erica was a little disconcerted that Jenny wasn't her usual enthusiastic self at the first conference. "The next few hours," she'd told Jenny, "should be valuable ones for you; we'll be running into things you haven't run into before."

Jenny nodded absently and Erica repressed a feeling of irritation. She'd told Jenny she was executive material, but the girl didn't seem overjoyed with her learning experience.

"What's the matter?" Erica asked her as they were leaving the first appointment and heading for one of the in-store boutiques. Erica had her eye on an assistant manager at the Hideout there who might be just the woman to manage the Quincy Market store.

"Oh . . . Paul phoned last night."

Erica thought: I've just about had it with Paul. She had a very Josh-like impatience with personal matters when her mind was set on business. Besides, maybe she and Jenny had talked enough; maybe the other woman needed some time to think this through herself.

"I see. Well, I'll tell you what, Jenny, why don't you take off now and go around on your own this afternoon? I'll see you back at the hotel . . . whenever, probably around seven?"

She couldn't conceal the impatient edge to her voice, though she tried, and she noticed that Jenny looked a little hurt.

"Okay. Are you sure it's all right?" Jenny brightened, looking a bit guilty at the same time.

"Sure it is." Erica softened. She might be missing out on her own free time, but she *had* hinted that this would be something of a pleasure trip for Jenny, too.

It was no accident, Jenny thought, that she had chosen the "Freedom Trail" as her way of passing the afternoon. Much as she loved Erica and valued her job, Jenny had felt a certain reluctance and constriction today, a sudden distaste for business. Of course, it was because of the call last night. Paul had sounded so lonely and contrite—saying how desperately he missed her already—that Jenny's heart had melted.

She missed him, too, missed him awfully. And she wanted to go back to New York. She just hadn't been able to face telling Erica that, though, not yet. For the moment she needed the liberty of solitude, the time to think things over.

And the Freedom Trail had a pleasing and appropriate ring to it.

The little book she'd bought on Boston said it was "the one walking tour everyone must take." The trail was composed of sixteen numbered historical sights in a four-square-mile area of downtown Boston and Charlestown, requiring two or three hours to cover.

Jenny wasn't sure she had that much time to spare—everything took longer in a strange town—but there were certain sights she wasn't going to miss.

It was on Boston Common that she decided to take the bull by the horns and tell Erica she wanted to return to New York, skipping Philadelphia and Washington. Finding that more time had passed than she realized, she omitted a visit to the Paul Revere House and hurried on to her main destination—the Boston Tea Party ship and museum, an attraction that closed at dusk.

There Boston's most famous protest was dramatically presented in a museum and recreated aboard a full-scale working replica of the ship. The brig *Beaver II* was moored near the Congress Street Bridge, and Jenny boarded eagerly. She learned that visitors could relive history by throwing tea chests overboard—which were later retrieved by their rope harnesses—just as the original patriots had done during the first Boston Tea Party. It was just what she needed to relieve her nervous frustration and her anxiety about a possible conflict with Erica.

She joined a crowd of schoolchildren engaged

in the same activity; there were few adults aboard this afternoon aside from several who she assumed were teachers or parents. One man in the group seemed unlikely to be either; he was tall and strong and casually but expensively dressed in tight dark trousers, a striped turtleneck sweater and a leather jacket. He looked more like an adventurer, a sailor, than anything else and Jenny wondered what he was doing on this tame excursion. He had very darkly tanned skin and light, strange eyes.

She hoisted a tea chest and threw it over the side while the children around her clapped and cheered. Suddenly she had a vivid picture of Paul and it tore her heart; she was having fun, so far away from him, and he was struggling along with his classes and his boring job, coming home to a lonely apartment.

She was so sad that she burst into tears. As she stood at the rail the tears rolled silently down her cheeks.

The tall dark man who had been leaning negligently against the rail, surveying the scene with amusement, walked over to Jenny and took out a large white handkerchief. "Here," he said abruptly in a low, growling voice.

"Thanks." She blew her nose, feeling foolish, then started to hand the handkerchief back, but he said, "Keep it." After a moment he asked, "Want to talk about it?"

She looked at him uncertainly. He grinned and his teeth were dazzlingly white in his dark piratical face. "It's all right. I'm not trying to pick you up. I'm spoken for. And besides, you're wearing a wedding ring. Is your husband the problem?"

She stared at him. "Yes," she admitted. And all of a sudden she found herself talking to him openly and with a peculiar freedom, telling him about herself and Paul and the job.

"This boss of yours," he commented. "She's one of those hard-boiled career types, is she?"

"Oh, no! She's not like that at *all*. She's . . ." Jenny started to say Erica's name, but some feeling of caution stopped her. Instead she concluded, "She's young and beautiful and a very sweet person."

Jenny saw a quick brightness in the tall man's unusual eyes. "But I take it she's not married."

"No. She's a little . . . married to her job." Jenny felt disloyal and added, "I shouldn't have said that. In fact, I don't know why I'm telling you all this." She smiled ruefully.

"Because it's easier to talk to strangers. I always think so."

"I guess it is."

"You know what I think you should do, for what it's worth?"

"What?" Jenny asked.

"Go back to New York tonight. Go back and be with your husband. It's a hell of a thing to be lonely." Jenny thought the man sounded very lonely himself. "Take my advice," he added. Then after one more quick look around the ship and the wharf he raised his hand to Jenny in a casual farewell and disembarked.

* * *

Erica's watch showed ten after seven when she got into the elevator at the Copley. Her cocktail conference with a local financial writer had left her not much wiser about the irritating puzzle of Kimren. The papers that morning had contained nothing about it, but the Kimren stocks were now listed and had already reached a high value. The value of Warren stock had increased as well; she wondered how much of that was due to the Kimren situation.

Her mind was busily engaged with the problem when she entered the suite, but she wasn't surprised to see Jenny dressed for travel, standing with her packed bag in the living room.

"You're going back," she said blandly. Noting the nervous look on Jenny's face she added, "It's all right, Jenny. It really is. I know you're in a bit of a crisis situation, so it's no good for you to make the rest of the trip. You wouldn't get much out of it, anyway."

Jenny seemed on the verge of crying. "Oh, Erica, I don't want you to think this means I'm not crazy about the job. You know I love everything about it."

"Except being this far away from Paul." Erica grinned, then made a wry face that brought a smile to Jenny's anxious eyes.

"Yes. You *do* understand, don't you?"

"I really do." Erica kicked off her shoes and sat down on the couch. "Would you like Harry to drive you?"

"Oh, you're so good to me." Jenny bent over and hugged her. "No, thanks, I'm taking the airport limousine. You know, the weirdest thing happened this afternoon." Quickly she told Erica about her adventure.

"So this matchmaker advised you to desert me?" Erica asked with mock sadness. "What did he look like?"

Jenny described him.

I don't believe this, Erica reflected. It couldn't be anyone else. What on earth is he plotting now?

"Oh, that reminds me," Jenny said. "I have a little souvenir for you." She picked up a small box from the coffee table and handed it to Erica.

Opening it Erica saw the tiny replica of the *Beaver II.* "It's charming," she said. "Thank you very much." A sudden picture of the *Sereia,* riding at anchor in New York harbor, assailed her and she was bedeviled by the memory of Steven Kimball hauling her out of the water. So the captain of the *Sereia* had been on a busman's holiday.

"Well," Jenny said awkwardly, "I . . . I guess I'd better be going. Thank you, Erica. Thanks for understanding about this and for bringing me this far." She grinned and kissed Erica on the cheek. "I'm going to get everything straight, once and for all."

"Good." Erica put her arms around Jenny and hugged her. "Go on, now. I'll check with you tomorrow from Philly."

"Right." Jenny picked up her light bag and left the suite.

Suddenly all of Erica's irritation and disappointment were gone. She'd been impatient at the intrusion of Jenny's private life on their business, disappointed that she was showing an unprofessional attitude. But now all she felt was lonely and even a bit inadequate. Jenny was hurrying home to someone she loved, someone who loved her. And Erica Warren was by herself in a hotel room with an empty evening stretching before her.

She shook off the fruitless mood of self-pity, thinking: Nonsense. This won't get me anywhere at all. She had a dozen friends in Boston and Cambridge she could call. There was no need to be alone.

Briskly she went into her bedroom, took off her daytime ensemble and hung it up. Then she took a long, luxurious bath and washed and blew-dry her hair.

She zipped herself into a high-necked cream-colored robe and ordered a light dinner to be sent up to the suite, deciding to look over the Philadelphia and Washington plans while she ate.

But somehow the papers seemed redundant and wearisome. She knew Philadelphia, if anything, even better than Boston, and her business in Washington was the least pressing on her itinerary.

Erica shoved the papers aside and, after having the dishes removed, made a couple of calls. It was a little late in the day to make engagements, but she had two single friends, at least, who might be available for a cocktail and a visit.

To her slight dismay neither of them was at home, so she decided on an impulse just to go out by herself, something she almost never did.

She was haunted by a remark of Steven Kimball's about her acting like the heroine of a nineteenth-century novel. She felt wild and adventuresome, with the need to prove she wasn't like that.

Maybe she'd even meet someone. Other women did, every day, and the world didn't end. Maybe, Erica thought, I'll let go a little bit for once.

She went to the closet and took out an ensemble she hadn't yet had the nerve to wear: a two-piece evening pants set of copper metallic cloth, quite startling with her coppery hair. The top had a tight ruffle for a collar and long sleeves with matching ruffles at the wrists; it was cut tunic-style, fitting her upper body with becoming frankness. The softer trousers were gathered at the ankle. She put the ensemble on, donned matching copper sandals and chose a harmonizing shoulder bag.

When she emerged from the elevator in the Copley lobby she could feel the stares; it was as if she had become someone else, not her usual conservative self, and the idea made her reckless and jubilant.

She was acquainted with the Boston night life and decided to dare it that evening. She was annoyed to see a black Jaguar illegally pausing in the taxi area and, feeling belligerent and independent, came within an ace of telling the driver to move.

But deciding not to be foolish, she flagged a cab. Calling out the name of a neon-lit disco near Fenway Park—not at all her usual sort of place—she got in. She thought she saw the offending Jag pull out after her cab, but lost sight of it in the heavy traffic.

Erica paid the driver in front of the disco on Lansdowne Street. Glancing back, she saw no Jaguar in evidence before she entered the building. She was escorted to a small table for one and ordered a cocktail.

"Hello, again." She looked up when she heard the familiar voice.

"Oh, no," she said. "I'm being haunted. This could hardly be a coincidence."

"Anything but," he retorted. "I followed you from the Copley, but I beat you here. You had a very slow driver. May I?" Without waiting for her answer he reached over and pulled a chair from another table and sat down.

In light of their last encounter his sheer effrontery left her momentarily speechless. He acted as if they'd parted no more than ten minutes ago on the friendliest terms. Despite herself, Erica was strongly aware of his physical magnetism; she could feel the pull of his presence across the small table.

She thought: He takes a great deal for granted, almost as if we had had a date. If he thinks he owns me because of a few kisses, what would happen if he made love to me? She was thankful that nothing more had happened; apparently women always fell at his feet and he was spoiled rotten. Well, it wasn't going to happen with *her*.

His silvery eyes took in her face and hair and wandered over the shining form of her body beneath the metallic fabric. "You look like fire," he said, and the unexpected softness of his tone, the intimate sound of his voice, took her completely by surprise.

She felt a treacherous warmth stealing over her, a fluttering excitement in her core, and she realized fully just how overpowering he was, leaning forward staring at her, his powerful hands flat on the small table. She took in the amazing breadth of his shoulders, the biceps that strained the dark cloth of his jacket, the tanned, muscular throat that made such a striking contrast with the white open-necked shirt.

Erica tried not to look at his face, but found her gaze straying to his firm, arrogant mouth, his stubborn chin and fine aquiline nose. Slowly she looked up, still avoiding his eyes directly, noting the black swoop of his brows, the thick lock of hair that had slipped down over his brow.

"Look at me," he commanded. "Why can't you look me in the eye, Erica?"

At once her pride was stung. She stared defiantly into his silver-gray eyes, determined not to look away first. But he outstared her; those eyes were too powerful, too probing. Defeated for the moment, she looked down.

"Would you like to dance?" His sudden question, as unexpected as everything he'd said before, again put her off balance. She could hardly keep up her defenses when he constantly attacked her from so many different angles.

Automatically she said yes.

He rose and pulled out her chair for her, an almost old-fashioned gesture that perversely pleased her in spite of her usual disdain for most such mannerisms. On the dance floor she moved into his arms and he drew her close; his size, his muscularity and the power in his strong arms made her feel small, fragile and somehow precious. And the nearness of his body was overpowering. She felt her senses betray her. She closed her eyes, losing herself in the uncharacteristically soft music, leaning against him, relaxed and melting, following his firm leading steps with an almost dizzy lightness, as if she had turned into mist and water.

He was so tall that she only reached his collarbone; she turned her head slightly and her nose brushed the tanned skin between the wings of his open collar. Her heart hammered; she felt warm and helpless. He bent his head until his chin touched her hair, and, uneasy, she was aware that his lips were caressing her temple.

For a timeless moment she forgot all the unpleasantness that had passed between them, forgot his rudeness and arrogance and all his sly maneuvers in regard to Warren. Their slow steps melded in a lyrical perfection, a dreamlike harmony, and he moved closer and closer. She could feel his beating pulse, his tense excitement, the firm contours of his strong, massive body. Her blood sang in her ears like a frantic captured bird; her heart was pounding like the sea.

"Erica, you know what you want," she heard him say softly. "You know what we both want. Come . . . come with me. Let's get out of here." He was leading her from the floor and, almost hypnotized, she was letting him lead her.

She looked up into his face and was chilled by the look in his eyes—calculating, bright, triumphant. There was a cool half-smile on his lips.

Steven Kimball always got what he wanted, she thought. And for the moment it was her.

"No," she said sharply. "No." Quickly she returned to the table. With an unreadable expression he followed and sat down opposite her.

"May I get you a fresh drink?" he asked casually, showing no emotion at all. Contrarily she was nettled. It was all a game to him, after all.

"Why did you follow me to Boston . . . and how did you know where I·was?" she demanded, determined to be as indifferent as he.

He answered the last question first. "I have friends everywhere . . . and friends of friends." George, she thought; somehow it was connected with George, who knew her itinerary, and Arabella. "As to the why—I don't like to be thwarted. I've never known a woman quite so difficult as you. It adds a certain spice to the contest." His voice was light and mocking and he grinned.

Contest. The word confirmed everything she feared. Love was a game to Steven Kimball, the sportsman; she was no more than an evasive doe or a skittish horse to him.

"I expected to see you on the *Beaver II* today—hoped I might even have the chance to haul you out of the drink again. But I only ran into your assistant."

"Jenny?" she asked, amazed. "But how did you . . . how did you know who she was?" He *was* the man Jenny had described, then.

"I know a great deal. I saw you two on the street together and added two and two."

"And it was because of your advice that she went back to New York," Erica said tartly.

"Of course," he answered in a bland voice. "I thought it would be more fun if you didn't have a roommate."

She was furious at the implication. "And you assumed, of course," she retorted, her voice trembling with indignation, "that I'd fall into your arms."

"Well, didn't you?" He smiled at her wickedly. "You fell into them beautifully when we were dancing. I really didn't know you had it in you . . . aside, that is, from that splendid performance in the garden that night."

She pushed back her chair and got up. "As far as I'm concerned we're just competitors, Mr. Kimball. And I'm still going to get to the bottom of your Kimren ploy."

He rose, too, but he was still smiling his maddening smile. "Erica, Erica." He shook his head. "Kimren's becoming an obsession with you. Don't you ever take any time off from work?"

"I can't afford to," she countered. "There are too many sharks in the water."

"Water again," he commented, laughing. "You really know how to dampen a fellow's ardor, Miss Warren," he punned.

"Well, don't hold your breath, Steven Kimball. I hope the next time we meet it'll be in court. I have a strong feeling you're doing something totally illegal. And I just can't wait to find out what it is."

She fumbled in her purse and threw a bill on the table.

"I have it," he said curtly and she was amused to see how much she had annoyed him.

"I buy my own drinks, thanks." She flounced out of the room; Kimball cursed softly and followed.

On the street she signaled in vain for a taxi.

"Don't be foolish," he said with a condescending gentleness. "You're much too pretty to run around at night alone."

"I'll scream if I need you," she answered in a sarcastic way. Just then a taxi slowed and she got in.

"You will, Erica. You will," he called out as the cab drove slowly away.

Chapter Six

𝓔rica was dismayed to discover that Kimball's parting words lingered in her mind. Throughout the two days of her brief stay in Philadelphia she found herself with a sudden distaste for business; she didn't feel creative at all.

Instead of scouting for new boutique locations Erica settled quickly for another Erin Hideout in the Gallery at Market East, a multilevel shopping complex built around a sunken arcade and a glassy atrium, and another in New Market, centered around a man-made waterfall. The complexes were beautiful, the locations perfect, yet she felt she'd missed a bet in the suburbs. However, she was strangely languid and perfunctory. That was that.

Feeling restless, strange and unlike herself, Erica went back to her hotel. She entered her light-green suite, tossed her handbag onto a sofa and kicked off her high-heeled pumps. She sat down at the Louis XIV writing table and took some papers from her portfolio. She was busily making notes on some new ideas for Washington and Miami when the Princess phoned purred.

A little impatiently she answered.

"Erica?" It was Morgan Hunt.

"Morgan," she replied without enthusiasm. "Are you calling from New York? You sound so near."

"I *am* near." He laughed, sounding warm and excited. "I'm on the house phone downstairs."

She was silent so long that he asked anxiously, "Are you still on the line?"

"Yes." A vast impatience overtook her. What on earth was he doing here? Was he still pursuing her?

"May I come up?"

"No," she said sharply. "No, I'll come down."

"Have you dined?"

"No." Oh, no, she thought. I should have said yes.

"Then let's go out to dinner, shall we?"

She hesitated. Repressing a sigh she finally answered, "Very well. I'll be down in ten minutes or so."

When she emerged into the lobby he was waiting with an eager expression, immaculately dressed in a lightweight suit the color of cocoa that, she had to admit, looked very nice with his tanned skin and blond hair.

"Erica. You look wonderful."

"Hello, Morgan," she said so coolly that he looked dashed. However, he started to chatter with determined cheerfulness as they left the hotel, asking her if she'd enjoy one of the city's fanciest restaurants for dinner.

Erica knew that it was necessary to make reservations two days in advance, even on weekdays.

"I made the reservations from New York," Morgan commented, smiling at her look of surprise. "We have a lot to talk about. I wanted it to be somewhere quiet and special."

"You were very sure I'd accept," she remarked.

"No." He looked serious. "I took the chance. I do thank you for coming."

"Quiet and special" was hardly the right description, Erica reflected with amusement as they entered the little brownstone on Pine Street. The room was like a French opera set, with its love seats, banquettes and Empire chairs upholstered in deep rose and touches of fern green and pink everywhere.

Morgan studied her admiringly. "I think you're more beautiful than ever. Running off has agreed with you."

Suddenly she realized that "running off" was just what she had done; in her heart she knew that the trip had been an excuse to run away—from Morgan, from herself. And she remembered what Steven Kimball had said: that she was afraid to be a woman.

She made some casual reply, glad that Morgan was so absorbed in choosing a wine that he hadn't seemed to notice her expression. Sitting across the table from him perversely reminded her of Kimball; the contrast between them was so great. And she could not help recalling the quick, savage kisses in the museum garden, the piercing silvery eyes in the Boston disco.

Erica found her appetite fading, but again Morgan appeared not to notice. He was chattering away about New York acquaintances and casual matters. Nevertheless she knew he was leading up to something.

She was toying with a dessert of frozen grapes and sipping the superb coffee when Morgan's look turned serious. She took the initiative, asking bluntly, "What brings you here, Morgan?"

He set down his coffee cup and reached across the table to take her hand. She withdrew it quickly and he frowned. Then his brow cleared and he tried to smile. "You, of course. Have you changed your mind?"

"No, I haven't, Morgan. I'm sorry. I told you that it's impossible."

He looked downcast again. "All right. I'll accept that . . . for now. But there was something else I wanted to talk to you about, something I didn't want to go into on the phone."

"Kimren?" She raised her brows.

"Kimren. There are a lot of rumors on the Street right now about that mysterious little corporation. I imagine, knowing you, that you've kept up from out of town."

"Of course."

He looked surprised. "But what about yesterday's developments? How can you be so calm about that?"

Chagrined, she realized she had not been in touch with New York since she left Boston. She was caught off balance and was ashamed to let him know that.

"Because I'm working on it," she lied.

"But surely, now that George is involved . . . don't you think you ought to come back? It's a bad time to be away. If you wait too long Warren's is going to slip right out of your hands."

Good heavens, she thought, I've got to get hold of myself and get on this the first thing in the morning. She was feverish with impatience.

And suddenly she realized something else: Morgan's concern was not just on her behalf. He was worried about his own position. If they were married . . .

"And your hands, too," she said coldly, "if I were your wife."

Just for an instant he had a sheepish, annoyed look and she knew she had guessed right.

"But I'm not going to be your wife, Morgan. So it's very kind of you to be so protective of my interests."

"Erica . . ." He shook his head, sounding reproachful. "You do me an injustice. I came here hoping you would let me help you."

"It's all right, Morgan. I can handle it." She

was silent for a moment; then she decided to probe. "However . . . you're very close to George. How do you think he's going to jump?"

"Our friendship is a bit strained at this point, naturally," Morgan answered in a stiff, cool voice. "You must know that my loyalty can't be divided." He reached for her hand again and this time she let it remain in his.

"As much as it hurts me to say it, Erica," Morgan went on, "I think George is so resentful that he'd even let his own Warren stock slip away if it could harm your position. And I'm afraid Roger would go with him."

Erica was very uneasy. Could it be true— would George's resentment take him that far?

"And Merry *is* their mother, Erica."

"Merry?" Erica couldn't repress her amusement. "Merry would never go along with them, Morgan, never. Embarrassing as it may be, she knows what George and Roger are, even if they're her own sons. She's said so a hundred times." Erica was a little annoyed at herself for revealing so much. Apparently it was news to Morgan, because his blue eyes brightened and he said thoughtfully, "I see. I see."

Gently she withdrew her hand from under Morgan's and said, feigning tiredness, "You must forgive me, Morgan. I've had quite a day and I'll have another early one tomorrow. I'm off to Washington, then Miami. I'd better be getting back to the hotel."

She listened to his protests unmoved. Finally he shrugged and said, "All right. You win."

Signaling for the bill he added, "Remember, though, I haven't given up on you. Not yet."

At exactly nine the next morning Erica made several New York calls from the airport. None of her contacts, including a close friend on the Securities and Exchange Commission, had as yet unraveled the Kimren mystery, but two assured her that they were close.

Later that morning Erica settled into her suite in a fancy Washington hotel and eagerly sat down to read a long letter from Merry which had followed her all the way from Boston.

The letter sounded unlike Merry's forthright, self-sufficient style; she mentioned feeling a bit unwell and went into great detail about a disturbing conference with Roger and George. Her sons were pressing her to sell her Warren preferred stock; she was mystified about it all. What did Erica think? Merry asked in conclusion.

Erica went to the phone at once to call her aunt, who was out. She would have to try again later.

She set out on her errands with a heavy heart; for Merry to say she was a "bit unwell" could mean she was very unwell indeed. Meredith Blaine was famous for her cool understatement. And the maneuvers of George and Roger were not reassuring.

But she could do nothing about it at the moment, so she concentrated determinedly on the day's business, which was concluded without incident.

She was disturbed to find that Merry was still

out that afternoon; the housekeeper said she'd had a doctor's appointment. Despite being sharply questioned she could give Erica no specific information.

All that afternoon Erica was extremely distracted, transacting business with only half her attention. It was not until that night that she was able to talk to Merry, who made light of her indisposition but seemed eager to discuss the matter of Roger and George. Their long conversation reassured Erica a great deal. Nevertheless she later wrote Merry a long detailed letter, telling her about the trip and including all she had been able to learn about the Kimren situation. "Which isn't much at this point," she added wryly in the letter.

Finishing the letter to Merry, Erica promptly wrote an even longer one to Jenny, whom she had spoken to from Philadelphia. After she had finished her correspondence she suddenly felt an overwhelming sense of loneliness and fatigue. She longed for the next day's business to be concluded so she could get to Miami. There, she decided, she'd spend an extra day or so and just relax.

Georgetown, some distance from downtown Washington, had its own special character; Erica had always loved the brick streets and gracious old houses. Antiques and decorators were everywhere. An affluent and cultured crowd had begun to restore the town houses, discovering wide-plank floors and uncovering mahogany banisters and other treasures from under coats of enamel. As property prices shot up, a pub or two had opened.

With affluence came the boutiques and a new hotel or two. Now it was a "scene"—discos, bars, many new restaurants and shops full of chic clothes. It was just right for a new Erin location. Erica concluded her errands with dispatch, a little dismayed at her reluctance to look up her acquaintances in Georgetown.

She was in a restless and rather negative mood by two in the afternoon; it was a muggy day, quite warm for the time of year, and gray and overcast. And she could not quite forget her unsettling encounter with Steven Kimball in Boston. Unconsciously she had looked for him in Philadelphia and again in Washington—he had made it clear that their meetings so far had been no coincidence—and, what was worse, could not tell whether she felt relief or disappointment when he failed to appear.

Perhaps he had tired of the chase, she concluded. Even he, obstinate as he was, couldn't keep it up indefinitely. Right now, Erica concluded, she had to decide where to go to kill some time. She suddenly remembered a spot she'd always enjoyed—Dumbarton Oaks and Gardens. It was a beautiful sixteen-acre estate, once a country farm and now the home of Harvard's Center for Byzantine Studies, with two wonderful museums and enchanting public gardens. She recalled that it was usually open until five, so she had plenty of time.

Erica felt a new peace and contentment as she

wandered through the museum that housed a rich Byzantine art collection dating back to the sixth century. Lost in contemplation of the treasures she began to forget all the matters troubling her, even Merry's worrisome condition. And then suddenly, in one of the pieces, she thought she traced a resemblance between a dark exotic face and the face of Steven Kimball.

This is really too much, she thought, stricken. That man is haunting me. Her head was beginning to ache. Needing to get some air and to escape from the disturbing reminder she hurried out of the museum and made her way to the gardens.

She drew a breath of relief; the gardens were magical, winding gently down to Rock Creek Ravine and offering a serene retreat from the humid air with their half-hidden benches and secluded nooks.

She caught sight of one small enclosure and walked slowly toward it. She could just glimpse a bench that looked unoccupied, but when she reached it she saw that someone had gotten there before her.

"Erica." Steven Kimball stood up at once when he saw her, his light jacket carelessly hooked over his thumb. His lean hips and long legs were encased in tight-fitting dark-brown trousers. He looked easy and relaxed, in total command, as always, and she realized again what extraordinary magnetism he had. His face lit up and he smiled broadly. "We meet again."

Erica was on the point of saying, "You're following me again," but for some reason felt reluctant to do so. She longed to find some sharp, sarcastic retort that would put him in his place. Instead she just looked at him and sat down at the end of the bench.

"What's the matter, Erica?" he asked softly, sitting down beside her. For the first time since they'd met he sounded really concerned, not mocking. She was thrown off balance by the simple caring in his tone. It was hard to remember, at a time like this, that he wasn't a friend at all, only a wily opponent in the continuing battle for power. And the stakes were too high for her to relax her guard.

When he added in the same kind way, "You look . . . a little tired," she retorted sharply, "Thanks very much." And over his next protesting words she cut in with, "Just a bit of jet lag . . . a lot of business . . . and never being left alone long enough." She emphasized the last words.

"I think you've been left alone far too long," he countered and reached out to take her hand. She drew it away.

"And of course," she flared, "you're the one whose company I need to put things right—Kimball the Takeover King, also God's gift to all needy women, judging from that photograph." Erica could have bitten off her tongue; she'd never meant to mention that.

Glancing at him she saw a brilliant gleam in his silvery eyes. "Oh, *that*." He smiled a teasing, lopsided smile. "I'm surprised at you, Erica. You've been around enough to know how meaningless such pictures are. But I'm flattered that you remember it so vividly."

"Don't be ridiculous," she snapped. "It wouldn't matter to me if you had a hundred women around. Your giant ego is just a joke to me; it's your more . . . sinister activities that make me nervous."

"Sinister activities?" he repeated, grinning. "Why, goodness gracious"—he used the spinsterish phrase ironically—"what *do* you mean, Miss Warren? Drugs and gunrunning . . . starting revolutions?"

"You know perfectly well what I mean." She looked straight into his eyes. "It's your interest in Warren Industries, Mr. Kimball. Well, you're not going to get my company away from me." She saw the gleam in his eyes go out; they became flat, angry and hard, the color of a stormy sky.

"You know, Erica," he said in an exasperated tone, "I've been accused many times of loving money above everything else, of being in love with power. But, lady, you're a mile ahead of me in that area. I've never seen any woman, especially one so young and beautiful, so dedicated to grabbing the dollar and keeping her place as the queen bee. No, ma'am, you take the blue ribbon. Your obsession makes mine look like a whim."

She started to speak, but he held up one strong tanned hand and ordered, "No. Let me finish, for once, before you get up and run away, the way you did in New York and Boston. I have a few more words to say to you. Did it never occur to you that I might be on your side? That there might be more to all this business—and this damned mad chase—than you realize?"

She stood up, trembling with anger. "You have no right to talk to me like this. I realize plenty, Mr. Takeover; I realize that you want me simply because you can't get me . . . and you want Warren's for the same reason."

He stood up, too, and suddenly grabbed her in his powerful arms. "You little . . . shrew. You damned little shrew," he growled and, taking her face between his hands, he kissed her savagely.

When he released her she said breathlessly, "Why don't you quit following me now? You're going to lose both your battles—me and my company."

He dropped his hands and glared down into her eyes. "You've just about convinced me, Ice Princess. I'll just let Her Frigid Highness handle her own problems."

This time it was he who walked away. He turned on his heel and strode off down the winding path toward the ravine, leaving Erica standing there in a confusion of wild emotions.

Erica had calmed down a good deal by the time she reached Miami. She had scheduled her tour of the city's boutiques for the second day, so the first could be devoted to rest and sun. Checking the weather, however, she amended her plans to include a walk in the rain by the ocean, something she also enjoyed. If she had ever needed to unwind it was now, after that unpleasant meeting with Steven Kimball. Much as she loathed admitting it, it had galled her to hear him call her Ice Princess again. But as long as the sea was near, she thought, consoled, she could forget other things and loosen up. At the hotel she unpacked hurriedly and got into a casual top, duck pants and sneakers. Slipping on a long rubberized rain cape of bright gold she went out to the beach.

It was almost deserted on this rainy day; the southern Atlantic was not its usual sunlit blue-green. The gray-green immensity of it reminded her of the great somber waste of the northeastern ocean. She was sharply, inevitably reminded of Steven Kimball diving from the *Sereia de Madeira* into New York harbor. And the whole tangle of Kimren, the vastness of her responsibility at Warren, overwhelmed her. She had a deep, strange longing for a simpler, easier life, for the leisure and irresponsibility other women enjoyed.

She let her hood slip back and raised her face to the caress of the light rain, inhaling the scent of the sea. Steven Kimball had said someday she'd need him; did she need him—or some other man—now?

Erica realized that her hair was drenched and that the air had turned cool. She shivered.

"No," she said aloud, her voice utterly lost in the sound of the waves and the rising wind. "I don't need him or anyone else." She was tired, that was all. After she'd rested awhile she'd be raring to go again. And there was no way in the world she could live like other women—not now, anyway. There was too much she had to plan and do. Josh Warren had left Warren to her because he'd known that she *did* have a sense of responsibility, ambition and drive. Her doubts had been the product of a weak moment and she wouldn't let them overcome her again.

She made her way back to the hotel and through the elegant lobby, amused at the surprised stares of the people there. Here she was, the Baby Tycoon, the famous Erica Warren, trailing through the place like a water rat instead of sensibly staying indoors and having her hair done like the other pampered women.

She grinned mischievously at the elevator operator. At this unexpected sign of humanity, he grinned back, and by the time she got to her suite her sense of humor and of herself was restored.

Erica took a long hot bubble bath and then turned on the shower to wash her hair. She felt totally renewed. After a room-service lunch she started to make some phone calls. She had many friends in Miami, as in the other cities.

One of them, a former school friend who had married a Miami executive, was delighted to hear from her. "My dear!" Virginia Temple exclaimed. "You're just in time for my party. We're having it on the boat tonight, at nine or so. You must come. It should be fun, even with this mad weather."

The "boat," Erica was aware, was a fifty-foot yacht moored at Key Biscayne. She grinned. "I'd love it," she said. Hanging up, she reflected that this was just what she needed: people, distraction. It would lift her from her silly, morbid mood.

She spent a lazy and pleasant few hours reading and watching television, putting all business matters out of her mind. When it was time to dress she chose a soft soigné pants outfit that came in three parts: a sleek tunic and pants and a long shawl to drape over her right shoulder. The silk-jersey ensemble was chocolate brown with a watery flower print of blossoms the bright russet of her hair; the whole thing had a border trim of brown and metallic copper. It was high-necked and long-sleeved, yet anything but prim. The silk clung to her shapely breasts and subtly outlined her sensuous hips and long slim legs.

She let her hair flow free and put on long slender earrings of red-gold. With a small neat envelope bag of metallic copper the outfit was smashing.

She felt marvelous as she boarded the yacht and greeted her host and hostess. In a moment she was surrounded by other acquaintances and friends and she knew she was going to have a very good time.

As she moved along the deck with Virginia Temple she glimpsed a tall, dark man carelessly dressed in an open-necked white shirt cut full like a pirate's and slim dark pants. He was leaning on the rail with a plastic highball glass in his hand.

"Hello, again," Steven Kimball said.

Erica started and was chagrined to feel the sudden heat in her cheeks, the treacherous acceleration of her heart.

She took a deep breath and answered calmly, "Hello."

"You know each other then," Virginia Temple remarked with pleasure.

"Oh, yes, indeed." Kimball's answer was full of sly meaning and Erica was nettled at its intimate tone.

"How nice." Virginia Temple smiled at them and gave Erica a curious little glance.

"Virginia!" her husband called out. "Could you come here a minute, honey?"

"Of course," she responded. To Erica and Kimball she said, "Excuse me a minute, would you?"

"By all means, Ginny. You run right along." Kimball grinned wickedly and looked at Erica.

He tossed his highball overboard, glass and all, and took Erica by the arms. "So now I've got you again . . . for the moment."

She stood impassively in his grasp and said, despite the loud beating of her heart, "This is beginning to remind me of a bad movie. You keep turning up."

"Not such a *bad* movie, really," he retorted lazily. "The characters are good-looking; the setting is nice." He gestured toward the handsome guests, then at the shining waters of the bay; the moon had come out and cast its silvery glow on the deck and over the water.

She was embarrassed at the trembling of her voice when she asked, "Are you following me, Mr. Kimball?"

When he replied, "You forget that I have a few other things to do, Erica," she was even more embarrassed. But it was too much of a coincidence.

"Your timing, though, is quite remarkable," she retorted. She was relieved to find that some of her calm had returned; her voice sounded steadier. But she was uncomfortably aware of his strong magnetism, the power of his big body. And the piercing silver eyes in the deeply tanned face set her off balance, as always.

"Of course I'm following you, you silly woman." His voice took on a deep growling quality; again it affected her like the touch of hands on her skin and she felt a quick, excited heat rise deep within her, a trembling in her very core. "I'm waiting to catch you in something less concealing." His bright eyes swept her from head to foot. "You have a passion for hiding that gorgeous body." He looked her up and down again; it made her feel undressed.

She turned away with a restless movement and murmured, "If you'll excuse me I have to say hello to a lot of people."

"Not so fast. You've said hello; try good-bye." She saw then that they were alone on their part of the deck. With a swift motion he took her in his arms; then with one strong hand he lifted her chin and kissed her.

At the touch of his mouth Erica knew again that perilous, treacherous warmth and melting of her body, even while her sense and pride resisted. His nearness overwhelmed her; the hardness of his circling arms, the power of him dizzied her. She realized—uncaring in that one, wild moment—that her mouth was parting under his, her arms were stealing around his neck as he pressed closer and closer, her whole self was pounding with the hammering of her pulse in her ears.

Behind her closed lids was a wavelike pattern of shifting redness and dark; she was beyond thought, far beyond the bounds of time or reason as she melted against him and knew the demanding power of his desire.

Then slowly he released her, whispering, "Erica, Erica," sounding hoarse and breathless like a man after a long grueling race run as fast as the very wind. He looked down into her eyes and she was dazzled and helpless in the path of that blinding silver fire—brighter, more bewildering than the light of the round moon washing over them.

He raised his hand from her waist and stroked the side of her face with it, smiling at her, looking gentler and more joyful than she had ever seen him look before. "You see?" he asked softly. "Now we can take up where we left off, have what we lost before. You'll come with me this time, won't you, Erica?"

The unaccustomed softness of his tone, the silver light, the magical warmth of his hand upon her hypnotized her into dumb acceptance. There was no resistance in her anymore as she nodded, and a victorious brightness shone from his strange light eyes.

Without another word he took her hand and led her back along the deck to the gangplank. There no longer seemed to be any question of good-byes; courteous, conventional formalities suddenly had a wild absurdity in the dreamlike space this dark commanding man had made for them.

Still silent, they walked along the pier toward a parking area filled with shining cars, hearing the music and laughter behind them fade. He opened the door of a low-slung black car and handed her inside; trembling, she leaned back, smelling fine leather and a faint tobacco scent, then the clean musk smell of him as he got in beside her. Vaguely she was aware that they were speeding off into the night, across the causeway leading back to Miami.

Now and then he glanced at her swiftly out of the corner of his eye, a slight smile on his fine, arrogant mouth, then shifted his gaze straight ahead to the flashing road before them. She studied his profile in the passing lights—the stubborn jaw, the hawklike nose, the glittering eyes under their brows of craggy blackness. Her gaze dropped to his long muscular legs that strained the tight black trousers and rose again to his powerful hands, confident and sure on the steering wheel.

She shivered, recalling the touch of those hands, marveling that to look at them brought back the very feel of them.

He didn't ask her what was the matter and she felt he knew, and gloried in that knowledge, because her slight trembling caused him to lean a little toward her, although he didn't look at her.

When the black car drew up before her hotel she made no comment; somehow he always knew where she was staying, always found her, in whatever city she had been. There seemed to be no words now, anyway, that needed to be said; they had said them all before, with eyes and lips and hands.

An attendant hurried forward to open her door and help her out. Steven Kimball was at her side in a moment; in the brilliant light from the lobby of the hotel he gave her one protracted, meaningful look and led her in.

"Miss Warren!" The sound of her name jarred her; she blinked, like someone awakened from sleep. She was being called from the desk. Bemused, she walked over with Steven Kimball at her side.

A man handed her a yellow envelope. "Telegram for you," he said courteously and handed her her key.

She murmured her thanks and, absently holding the envelope in her hand, went with Steven to the elevator. The silent ascent seemed as dreamlike as the interval before and their emergence into the carpeted hall was so sudden and quiet that she felt as if she were floating, not walking, toward her suite.

Steven took the key from her and unlocked the door. They stepped into the luxurious room, dim with rosy light, and he shut the door swiftly with his foot, taking her savagely into his arms again. He kissed her deeply again and again and she felt her whole body turn to water and to fire. Leaning into him, against him, she returned his starved kisses with a strange new ferocity that she had never known. He gave a low-voiced, wordless cry and with stunning suddenness gathered her up in his arms and strode with her into the bedroom of the suite.

After kicking open the door he set her on her feet again. Then with swift hands and surprising gentleness he took her telegram and her small bag from her grasp, tossing both onto a chair.

There was only one small lamp lit in the room; by its light she looked up at him and with a blend of fear and longing saw how much he resembled a triumphant buccaneer. His black hair was ruffled and wild, a heavy lock falling over one bright eye. The buttons of his shirt had come undone and his tanned broad chest was almost bare; his feet were planted wide apart. The color in his dark face was high and he was smiling with excitement. The smile lent his mouth a sinister cast and his silver eyes seemed to be burning, burning into her, the way his hard hands had heated her helpless flesh with their barbaric magic.

For the first time she felt a protest, a reluctance rising in her, but he was too powerful a force to deny; already his massive hands were roughly tossing aside the silken shawl from her trembling shoulder, unfastening the tiny buttons of her tunic with speed and skill, drawing the soft trousers down over her hips, undressing her as if she were a child. He knelt down and unbuckled one of her brown shoes, slipping it off her foot, then repeating the process with the other. She stood before him in her filmy bronze chemise, her breasts plainly visible through the transparent net, her most secret body exposed now to his sight.

He stepped back and devoured her from head to foot with his piercing eyes. "Oh, Erica," he whispered. "Erica." He seemed unable to say more as he continued to stare at her slender trembling form.

Then he knelt down before her, to her astonishment and delight, his skilled mouth wandering up her long bare legs until it caressed the soft skin of her inner thighs. She was trembling so she could scarcely stand, thrilling to strange new sensations utterly undreamed of; she closed her eyes.

His knowing fingers were undoing her chemise. She felt the soft air on her naked skin as the fragile garment fell away. Now he was caressing her in a fantastic way that she had only read of, never dreamed of experiencing, and the hot waves of incredible pleasure began to spread from the center of her throughout her shuddering body. Her knees were shaking; she moaned and cried out, fearing she would fall, but his strong hands held her upright as she rode upon the cresting breakers of abandoned joy so overpowering that she was deaf and blind and numb in every sense but one and yet alive in every nerve, rising and rising with the rhythm of hot sensation, utter pleasuring. She cried out, sliding down in his embrace until she, too, knelt upon the floor.

She could hear his quick, excited breath as he scooped her up again in his massive arms and carried her to the wide bed. He laid her upon it with enormous care and tenderness, leaning down to kiss her face and neck and arms and body once again. For a second he was gone; she heard the rustle of clothes, hasty movements, and opened her eyes.

He was standing naked over her and the dark perfection of his body dazzled her languorous sight—his narrowness of waist, the breadth of arms and chest, the lean strength of his mighty legs. He was like the statue of a Roman gladiator she had once been enamored of, alone in a museum one rainy afternoon. The memory pierced her flesh; he was overwhelming, god-like.

Now he was with her, his powerful yet gentle hands again stroking her shuddering skin; their stroking brought forth new waves of wild, sweet hotness, greater trembling. To her amazement she was aroused once more to a desire beyond enduring, mere moments after the unutterable happiness she had known before. He muttered soft endearments to her, all the while kissing her, stroking her with his magical hands.

Her own untutored fingers began to respond, and as she touched him she felt him shaking, heard him crying out, and suddenly they were in the ultimate sweet closeness. She felt the rhythm of the sea in them, the rocking waves, and reached a tall place of blinding brightness, silent cries. For the first time in all her days she found a fullness and completion; all emptiness was ended. She heard his answering voice of wondering relief and joy and drifted with him downward to a quiet peace.

They lay together, wordless, marveling. He said her name at last in a stunned voice and held her tightly to his shaken body. When his hoarse, quick breathing slackened he said her name again and asked softly, "Did I . . . hurt you, my darling?"

"Hurt me?" she repeated, puzzled. Then with astonishment and tenderness she realized that he had not, saying quickly, "No. Oh, no." Dimly she recalled the slightest pain, no more than the sting of a bee, and thought: How wonderful, how remarkable that is, in itself.

They talked little after that, half-drowsing, half-awake for a timeless interval; the hours slipped away, immeasurable, unimportant, and there was nothing left for them but one another.

To her amazement their longing renewed itself again and yet again, and she found to her delight that she was more practiced, more at ease with each encounter, feeling his astonished pleasure, too. At last they fell into an exhausted sleep, close in each other's arms.

Sometime during the abandoned night, at an hour that felt like dawn, Erica awoke with a sudden uneasy awareness that there was something left undone. Slipping out of his arms she kissed his shoulder and his face. He smiled in his heavy sleep and she rose carefully from the bed.

The telegram.

The telegram could be from Merry or about her. Anxiously, with a thudding heart, Erica retrieved the yellow envelope and went with it into the sitting room. The sun was rising flame-red in the sky, dimming the artificial lights. She turned off the lamps and tore open the envelope. The telegram was from her friend on the SEC; it contained only three words: KIMREN IS KIMBALL.

Stunned, Erica stared at the yellow page. Then she crumpled it in her hand and sank down on the couch. The man who had made love to her, given her such indescribable pleasure during the mad, abandoned night, turning her into a trembling puppet helpless in his hands, was the same man who was a trickster, maneuvering to take everything she owned and held dear.

She felt weak with the pain of it; then a hot anger drove away the hurt and she thought: First my company, then me. I've been the ultimate takeover, just another in a series of his sexual prizes.

She had to get away at once. She had to leave before he woke; she couldn't face him, not ever again. Hastily she showered, dressed and made up. Then, soundlessly, without looking again at the man on the bed, she threw her clothes into her suitcases and, thankful that he continued to sleep heavily, closed the door to the suite with barely a noise.

She would not let herself think of him as the elevator descended to the lobby; determinedly she concentrated on all the practical things she had to do: change her flight to Dallas, send telegrams from the airport to explain the broken appointments in Miami and, at a civilized hour, phone New York.

She must hurry; he could wake at any moment. And it would never do, she thought angrily, for him to let his latest prey escape.

By the time Erica boarded her flight she was trembling with exhaustion. As the plane headed west she fell into a grateful sleep.

Chapter Seven

$\mathcal{E}$rica felt a light touch on her shoulder and woke abruptly.

"Hope I didn't startle you." The pretty flight attendant smiled at her. "We'll be coming into the Dallas–Fort Worth Airport in twenty minutes."

Erica thanked her and, feeling light-headed, rose and made her way to the bathroom to freshen up. Examining her face in the mirror she realized that she looked like a different woman. Despite the rush and fatigue of the hectic morning her eyes were bright and clear.

Yet there was a look in them, a depth there, that she had never seen before. And it was not her imagination that her lips had a new fullness; no, they were different, too. It was all because of that incredible magical night with Steven Kimball.

In an instant she was overcome with fresh pain. It had been the most beautiful, the most glorious night of her life. He had been tender and caring, bringing her the greatest happiness she had ever imagined. And she had run away. But how could she have done otherwise?

The brutal fact of the message in the telegram remained. There was no way around it. Steven Kimball was moving to take over Warren, to take her authority from her. And she had given herself to him, gladly and freely. The realization of her foolishness made her blood run cold, left her humiliated and drained.

Drearily she put her makeup back in her cosmetic case and dropped it in her capacious shoulder bag, thinking: What of it? Thousands of women, in these "enlightened" days, did what she had done and thought nothing of it. It was just another encounter for him, she was certain.

But for Erica Warren—that was another matter. She could not help clinging to the fiction that love and sex were irrevocably intertwined. Probably she would never change. And yet the most important experience of her life had been with a man who didn't love her. Steven Kimball hadn't spoken a word of love. He had wanted her; she had been a challenge. Now that the chase was over, she thought, she was probably just another woman to him.

And yet she was tortured by uncertainty. He had followed her all over the East, had made love to her with such sweetness and tenderness.

Erica tried to put the whole thing out of her mind as she rode the seventeen miles from the airport to downtown Dallas. As soon as she had checked into her hotel and been shown to her suite her mind was already occupied with the day ahead. It was late enough now both to call New York to check on Merry and to set up her Dallas appointments. She did so, happy to be reassured about her aunt's state of health and able to line up a number of local appointments despite the earliness of her arrival. Then she decided to give Jenny another call.

Jenny Landon had everything at her fingertips, ready for Erica's calls. Now, as she heard Erica's voice, she was totally prepared to report on developments at the office.

"How's Miami?" she asked warmly.

"I'm in Dallas." Jenny thought her employer's voice sounded a little tense—or sad, or something.

"Dallas! You're ahead of schedule. Is everything all right?"

"Fine." Erica's reply was crisp, discouraging personal questions. "I have a few things I'd like you to take care of."

Immediately Jenny's pen was poised over her notebook. "Right."

Erica directed that flowers be sent to Meredith Blaine by her regular florist and asked Jenny to get the address and phone number of a certain doctor and have them available later that day.

"What's new there?" Erica asked her then.

After Jenny had finished her summary of the latest events Erica said, "About that other thing"—Jenny knew she was talking about Kimren—"I know for sure now who's behind it."

"The 'Pirate'?" Jenny said, using their code name for Steven Kimball, as Erica had arranged in a letter.

"None other." Jenny thought Erica sounded unusually cool and hard. "I want you to keep on the alert," Erica added, "and report to me on everything—*everything* in that area, especially G.B."

Startled, Jenny recognized the implication that Erica's cousin, George Blaine, was involved, but all she said was, "Of course."

"Another thing: I'm in touch by phone, but I want to know how my aunt looks . . . to *you*. Make some excuse to go to the house. She's always there in the mornings at about nine-thirty. Say that I've asked you to pick up some papers from my rooms upstairs. There are plenty there and it doesn't matter which ones you take."

"Certainly. I'll do it today. She's not well, I take it. I'm sorry, Erica."

"She may not be. But you're the only one whose judgment I can trust right now. I'll talk to the doctor, of course. But I'd like to know how she looks to your eyes, Jenny."

A few minutes later they hung up. Jenny promptly ordered the flowers for Meredith Blaine and recorded the address and phone number of the physician Erica had inquired about.

She phoned the town house and, finding Mrs. Blaine still in, asked if she might come over to look for certain papers Erica needed.

Meredith Blaine, who liked her, was cordial. "Of course, my dear. Come ahead. Perhaps we can have some coffee together."

Pleased, Jenny replied that she would be delighted.

But when she returned from the errand she was not as pleased as before. She would have to tell Erica, she realized, that Meredith Blaine did not look well at all.

She was even less pleased to find George Blaine hovering over her desk when she returned to the office.

"This is my mother's doctor," he remarked, indicating the notation on her calendar.

Jenny was nettled; she could hardly ask a member of the board, "Why are you snooping around my desk?" but she certainly felt like it.

"Really?" she responded coolly. "Someone recommended him to me," she said mendaciously.

George Blaine lifted his sandy brows. Then he answered in a nasty, rude fashion, "He's much too rich for your blood, kiddo. Unless my cousin's making *you* a member of the board." His ensuing laugh was most unpleasant.

How I dislike that man, Jenny thought, but

she kept her expression polite and bland. "Can I do anything for you, Mr. Blaine?" she asked in a calmly professional tone.

"You certainly could. But you're married, unfortunately."

Jenny felt her face heat.

George went on. "Just checking on the mice while the cat's gone." He smiled his unpleasant smile.

"Oh, we're keeping busy, Mr. Blaine." Jenny looked significantly around her at the busy typists in the office beyond, then at the pile of afternoon mail on her desk. "If you'll excuse me, I'd better get to the mail," she hinted.

Finally he moved away. "Be seeing you, Jenny." He waved and walked out of the office.

Jenny wondered what was going on; George Blaine had never done anything like this before. She also wondered if he had been in Erica's office while she was out. She'd certainly report this strange little incident to Erica, who was planning to call back tonight.

Erica's anxiety over that night's report was offset the next morning by a reassuring telephone conference with Merry's doctor.

"Of course she doesn't look well," he agreed. "She's getting on, you know, and is always overdoing. I've told her so again and again. I wanted her to get away from the city for a while, but she insists that traveling is more tiring than staying home. She's not much for a change of scene." The doctor chuckled.

"She has a point," Erica averred wearily. She

herself had had a late night; after calling Jenny she'd gone out with some of the local Erin people until the wee hours. "But you say there's nothing organically wrong at present?"

"Absolutely nothing. At *present*," he emphasized. "But I can't recommend too strongly that she slow down."

"I'll do my best, long distance. But maybe she needs someone to ride herd on her close by."

"It wouldn't do any harm," the doctor said. "But I'm sure you're tied up there, my dear. Try not to worry."

"All right."

During her second day in Dallas, Erica took his advice, which was easy enough because there was a great deal of business to transact. On her second evening she was heartened by a call to Merry, who sounded much better, and by the fact that Jenny had nothing negative to report.

On her third day in Dallas the temperature was a truly unseasonable eighty. Erica wore one of her own Erin designs. It was a cloud-soft beautiful black ensemble printed with small circles of cocoa-brown.

Her lunch companion, a handsome and brilliant public relations woman named Margaret Grey, admired the outfit as they went in to lunch.

"You're creative as well as beautiful," the woman said with breezy bluntness. Erica in turn silently admired her quietly confident manner and self-sufficient appearance.

"Well," Margaret Grey said after they had

ordered cocktails, "you're causing a small riot here." She inclined her head discreetly, her sharp hazel eyes twinkling, to a table near theirs.

Puzzled, Erica glanced in that direction out of the corner of her eye. Six tanned and well-dressed Texans of various ages were politely giving her the eye.

"Perhaps you are, too," Erica said modestly. Margaret Grey was a good-looking, strikingly dressed woman. "I've heard a lot of good things about you, Miss Grey."

"Call me Margaret, please. And may I call you Erica?"

"Of course." She smiled at the public relations woman, wondering suddenly how old she was. It was very hard to tell.

"Twenty years older than you." Margaret's eyes twinkled again.

Erica blushed. "Good grief, am I as readable as that?"

Her companion laughed. "Only to me, perhaps. I've had a lot of practice. In my business you get to know people pretty well. Particularly men, heaven help us all," she concluded in a wry tone. She studied Erica for an instant and seemed about to say something, but she apparently changed her mind, then asked smoothly, "Shall we order?"

Erica nodded, and after they had done so, Margaret said briskly, "I have an idea I think you'll go for. That is, if you're not too limited in your ad budget."

"I'm not."

Margaret brightened and began to talk swiftly and with enthusiasm. Her plan was well-thought-out and she presented it in a succinct and interesting way.

"Why don't you put the whole thing in writing and get it to me at my hotel in Houston tomorrow? After that I'll be in Chicago." Erica smiled. "I'll leave the dates and addresses."

"No need. I have it here." Margaret handed Erica a leatherette folder.

"I like your style." Erica grinned and flipped open the folder. "Tell you what," she said. "I'll take this with me and check it over tonight."

Just then the waiter brought their lunch. After he had served them Margaret protested, "Tonight? A beautiful young thing like you, reading prospectuses on her last night in Dallas? Oh, my dear, don't take *my* path."

Erica cut into her filet mignon and asked curiously, "What does that mean?"

Margaret took a bite of her salad and answered slowly, "I may lose a marvelous client by being too frank, but here goes. Twenty years ago, when I was your age and *almost* as pretty, I said no to a man and yes to my ambition. And I've regretted it ever since."

"Regretted it?" Erica protested. "But you have everything, Margaret—independence, prestige, one of the finest reputations in the business. And you're still a lot prettier than I am," she said sincerely.

"Lord love you for a sweet liar." Margaret took

a sip of her tonic water. "It's meals like this"—she indicated the Spartan lunch and drink with distaste—"that keep me human-looking. But 'independence, prestige and one of the finest reputations in the business' sure ain't foot warmers on a winter night."

Erica laughed. "But surely . . ." she began.

Margaret shook her head, looking very seriously at Erica. "I'm laughing on the outside, as the old song goes, but you know I sometimes feel that despite all this success that life has passed me by. I hope you won't let that happen to you." Suddenly Margaret looked a little embarrassed. "Please forgive me if I was out of line. I don't know *what* prompted all that," she concluded.

Erica smiled at her warmly. "It's all right. My grandfather told me the same thing."

"Josh Warren," Margaret said. "Now there was a man. They don't make 'em like that anymore."

"Not many, anyway." Suddenly Erica thought of Steven Kimball.

"Ah . . ." Margaret remarked slyly, studying Erica. "Well," she said briskly, "to get back to business. We'll really have to find some macho villainous-looking male models, but with polish, for the ads I have in mind. That won't be easy, but I'm sure they exist. I saw a picture of Steven Kimball the other day; too bad we can't get someone like him."

Erica was sure that her expression must be giving her away; her heart was thudding in her throat. But apparently Margaret hadn't noticed anything, for her eyes were gazing into the middle distance dreamily. "Now *there's* a sweet account," she murmured and chuckled. "I'd like to handle his public *and* private relations, if you'll forgive the expression."

For all her discomfiture Erica had to laugh at Margaret's outspokenness. At the same time she wished they could get off the subject.

Misreading her expression Margaret said quickly, "I'm sorry; I must have sounded offensive."

"Not at all," Erica assured her quickly. "I'm a bit of a hermit, but not a prude."

"You and King Takeover." Margaret's expression was wry. "Of course he's better known here in Texas . . . I suppose because the media are a little less sharklike than in the East or on the Coast."

"Really?" Erica managed to sound politely disinterested.

"Oh, yes. But of course you know Kimco's very big in oil."

"Naturally I know something about Kimco. Who doesn't, these days?" Erica kept her voice friendly but assumed a brisker tone. "Well . . . I think I'd better get going, but we'll certainly keep in touch."

After she had paid the bill and they were leaving the restaurant, Margaret said, "You'll love Houston, if you haven't been there before. They call it the 'Gold Buckle of the Sun Belt,' and how right they are."

"I've been there once and I do like it. Some close friends of my grandfather's have a ranch near Houston—the Kerrs."

"The Everett Kerrs?" Margaret asked with a look of pleasure.

"Why, yes."

"Good heavens, I went to school with his wife. Please give them my best if you see them."

"I will; I plan to. And I will be in touch soon."

"Wonderful. I look forward to it." Margaret raised her hand in a friendly wave and hurried away.

Erica walked down the crowded Dallas street in the dazzling sun, glancing at the pretty well-dressed women and the tall tanned men in their fine suits and handsome Stetsons. She couldn't get Margaret's advice out of her mind. And the mention of Steven Kimball had disturbed her more than she cared to admit.

Erica stretched her long slender legs with a languorous motion and said to Louise Kerr, "Ummm, this is wonderful."

The sun was blinding on the blue water of the swimming pool at the Lazy K; Erica's eyes were shadowed by huge brown-tinted sunglasses. She was lying back in a metal chair with green chintz pillows, a great deal of her skin exposed in the russet bikini that was almost the shade of her hair. Glancing down at herself she was surprised at how much darker she'd gotten in only three days.

"If you ask me, honey, you need about a year of this," Louise Kerr retorted. She was lying in the chair next to Erica's, sipping a drink. Louise was a small deeply-tanned woman of fifty, with short-cut gray hair and a plain, good-natured face. Her slimness gave her body a young look; only her weathered face revealed her age. Although Erica had not seen them often, she and Everett were like family to her.

"I still can't get over you," Louise said, as she had often done in the last three days. "I know it's been a long time, but you're so pretty and grown-up I still can't believe it. But, child, you're as skinny as a rail. You looked so tired when you first came and now you're getting all . . . smoothed out." Louise smiled with affection. "I wish we could persuade you to stay awhile."

"Good heavens, Chicago's on its ear *now,*" Erica protested. "I was due there yesterday." She thought: This *has* done me good, though. Her last day in Dallas had been hectic and she'd worked until late into the night.

The next morning's early flight to Houston and her two busy days in the city had further depleted her energy. When she had phoned Louise and been pressed to visit the Lazy K she had gladly accepted. But the visit, which she had intended to last only one day, had now stretched into three. She was resolved to get to Chicago the day after tomorrow, but at the moment she was reveling in her leisure.

"You're so much like your granddaddy, I mean in the way you go at things, that it's just unbelievable," Louise remarked.

"I guess I am. You know, it's always fascinated me that Granddad and Everett were so close in spite of the difference in their ages," Erica said thoughtfully.

Louise grinned. "Well, Everett always said your granddaddy had more steam than most men half his age." After a moment or two she added almost timidly, "I sure am glad that doggoned boat business got settled. That was a mighty bad time for us. It nearly broke my heart."

"I know. I was pretty young at the time, but I do remember something about it." Erica thought back. Seven or eight years ago her grandfather and Everett Kerr had become temporarily alienated over an offshore drilling project that conflicted with a Warren marine contract for the same area. Erica no longer recalled all the details, but she did remember being glad it came out all right because it had made their contacts with the Kerrs awkward.

"You'll never guess who owns that property now, Erica. That young boy there's so much talk about, the Kimco fellow."

Kimco again, Erica thought. Steven Kimball. Is there no place left where I won't hear his name?

"Steven Kimball," Erica said through stiff lips.

"That's the one. He offered Everett so much he just couldn't afford to turn it down. It built this pool, for one thing." Louise chuckled.

"Well, I'm glad it did," Erica rejoined lightly.

Louise studied Erica. "You're working mighty hard these days, little girl. How about changing your mind and staying with us awhile longer? I know some mighty good-looking boys who'd be thrilled to death if they could meet you."

"I really do have to leave soon, much as I'd like to stay." Erica passed over the comment about the "good-looking boys." She sat up in her chair and asked, "Would you mind if I borrowed one of the horses? I'd really love a ride before dinner."

"Of course not, honey," Louise said hospitably. "You go right ahead."

Erica kissed her on the cheek and went into the house to change into a shirt and jeans. Then she went down to the stables where one of the men saddled a gentle mare for her to ride.

She was glad of the solitude for the moment, glad to be away even from well-meaning Louise, with her passion for matchmaking. As she cantered over the long sweeping fields, watching a huge peaceful herd of cattle grazing in the distance, Erica felt an unaccustomed serenity.

For a time she toyed idly with the idea of what it would be like to marry one of the tall young ranchers the Kerrs would introduce her to and live in the luxurious quiet of this vast country.

Almost as soon as she thought it she was amused at her own nonsense; the bustle and hurry of cities were in her blood. As for marrying—there was no one she could dream of marrying now because she realized that Steven Kimball, like cities, was also in her blood. That dark conviction shattered her peace and she felt a quick, sharp yearning for him again and was ashamed at the same time of that very yearning for a man who was probably incapable of love.

She turned back abruptly and headed for the Lazy K. By the time she reached the ranch house it was almost dinner-time and she saw that Everett Kerr had returned from the city and was sitting by the pool in his broad cowboy hat, denim trousers and shirt sleeves.

"Hi, there," he called out, smiling when he sighted Erica. He set down his drink on one of the metal tables and stood up—a tall rangy man who towered over his small wife. "Have a nice ride?"

"Wonderful." Erica kissed him on his seamed cheek, warmed by the affectionate light in his farseeing blue eyes.

"Want to wet your whistle?" he asked companionably, gesturing toward the tray of drinks on a table.

"Not right now, thanks. I'll just sit a minute before I go upstairs. Where's Louise?"

Everett sank down again into his chair. "She's in the house getting dolled up for dinner." The outdoor extension buzzed. "Excuse me," he said and went over to answer it.

Erica leaned back in a chair and closed her eyes, catching snatches of his conversation. She heard him say, "Well, I declare. How're you doing, boy?"

Everett's deep voice reached her clearly. She heard a note of caution enter it and began to feel a little uncomfortable. Obviously he was having a conversation that he wanted to keep private, because now he was speaking in a kind of noncommittal staccato fashion.

"You don't say. Well, that's . . . interesting news."

Erica got up and saw him looking at her. She gave him a casual wave and headed for the door to the house.

"I don't know. I can't say," she heard as she went in. "I don't think so, but I can sure try, boy. I can sure try."

At dinner Erica noticed that Everett looked a little sheepish—not his usual open, bluff self. She wondered what was going on, and whether it had something to do with her.

With great casualness—too much casualness, she judged astutely—Everett asked, "Think we could twist your arm and get you to stay on the rest of the week?"

Somehow Erica had the feeling that his question related to the phone call. She answered, "I'd love it, I really would. But I must get to Chicago day after tomorrow. I really must."

"That's a shame. Are you real sure, now?" Everett exchanged a quick glance with Louise.

"Very sure, I'm afraid."

"Doggone it," Everett said. "We'd been planning all kinds of to-dos for Friday and Saturday."

"I'm really sorry," Erica said again, feeling a little pressed. "Next time," she promised, smiling.

Everett glanced at Louise again. He was so transparent, Erica thought. It was obvious that there was something in the wind. Probably, she reflected with amusement, it had to do with another one of the young men they'd picked out for her.

She was still puzzling about the matter after dinner, when they were watching the Kerrs' giant color television in the vast living room.

Erica was so preoccupied with the small mystery that it was very hard to follow the movie, which, in any case, was not one of her favorites to begin with. In the near distance, over the dramatic music of the television movie, she heard the sound of a copter touching down. Shortly after came the roar of a car approaching the house up the long, straight drive.

Oh-oh, she reflected. One of the Kerrs' presentations—another one of the young lean "good ol' boys" they were so eager to pair her off with. Erica stiffened a little. After Miami her friends' well-meant efforts were just too much to cope with.

She glanced at Everett. He looked, as Louise would put it, "as guilty as a sheep-killin' dog." She repressed a grin when he met her eyes.

"Sounds like we have company, Lou," he said to his wife in the same rather unnatural voice he'd used at dinner.

"Sure does. Wonder who it is?" Louise seemed sincerely curious. Evidently, Erica judged, she wasn't in on the "surprise."

Everett turned down the TV and they heard the maid at the door. "Good evening, Mr. Kimball."

Erica felt her face grow fiery; she hoped against hope that Louise and Everett hadn't been looking at her. But Louise seemed to be studying her covertly, with great interest. She tried to compose her expression.

When Steven Kimball strode through the archway into the room she wondered if she'd be able to meet his eyes. She recalled every moment of that night in Miami and suddenly her face felt hotter than ever, and her clothes so thin that she might have been naked before them all. She dug her nails into her palms, hoping to gain some control.

"Why, Steve!" Louise Kerr hugged him and when she released him Everett pumped his hand.

"Louise . . . Everett! It's really good to see you." Steven was grinning from ear to ear and his voice sounded warmer and more affectionate than Erica had ever known it to be. He really likes these people, she thought. It seemed unlikely that the arrogant Steven Kimball would befriend the Kerrs. And she realized something else—he looked handsomer, more appealing than ever. With a sinking feeling she stared at him, admiring his tall rugged leanness. The western clothes he wore suited him perfectly. She couldn't help comparing him to the other city men who wore them so absurdly. He looked as if he'd been born here, just as he seemed to be a born sailor. Above the light-gray shirt and trousers his black hair seemed night-dark in contrast and as always the silver-gray eyes were dazzling in his deeply tanned face.

He said, with a rather forced movement of surprise, "Why, Erica! This is a pleasant surprise." At last she made herself meet his silver stare and saw a look of mischief on his face. "I didn't know *you'd* be here."

Before she could answer Louise exclaimed, "Why, you two already know each other. How nice."

"Sure they do," Everett blurted. Then he looked sheepish.

Louise gave him a glance of mock reproach. "Everett . . . ?"

"This is wonderful," Steven was saying, keeping his piercing look on Erica. "Old home week all around." He came to Erica and took her hand. Dismayed, she had a sensation of electric heat at his touch. "I'm glad I . . . caught you," he added ambiguously. "Thought you'd be in Chicago by now."

She murmured something about being a little behind schedule, hoping her eyes and her flaming cheeks wouldn't give her totally away. She'd never been so uncomfortable in her life. It was as if his very presence recalled the wild intimacy of their night of love—and yet, she reminded herself, she wasn't at all sure it had been a night of love for him.

"Well, I *am* in luck." Steven wouldn't turn his relentless eyes away from hers.

Everett cleared his throat. "Can I, er, get you something? A drink? Have you had dinner?"

"I've had dinner, thanks, but a bourbon would go down fine." Erica noticed that Steven's very speech seemed plainer, his manner quite relaxed. He obviously felt completely at home with the Kerrs. For some strange reason this filled her with even greater confusion; it was hard to imagine the straightforward Kerrs being close to someone as unscrupulous as Erica believed Kimball to be.

Everett said to the women, "Ladies?"

Louise declined but Erica nervously asked for a glass of sherry. To her dismay Steven was the one who brought it to her while Everett was pouring his own whiskey.

"Thank you." She spoke in a very low voice and her hand trembled when she took the glass from Steven's hard brown fingers. She was relieved when he walked back to the bar to get his bourbon from Everett.

"Sit down, boy, sit," Everett urged him hospitably. Steven took a chair near Erica's; she was thankful she wasn't sitting on a sofa, because she wasn't at all sure she could sit so near him. Not tonight. She couldn't help noticing that he was observing her out of the corner of his eye even while he began calmly talking business with Everett.

Erica fervently hoped that they wouldn't be left alone together. She wanted to forget that Miami had ever happened and cursed the happenstance of her still being here.

She heard Steven saying, "No, I've got to stick around another few days. I've got some commitments in Dallas."

Just then the phone in the hall rang and the maid came in to tell Erica that it was a New York call for her.

She rushed to answer. It was her housekeeper, Hattie, who told her anxiously that Merry had been taken to the hospital and was in Intensive Care. She had had a stroke.

For an instant Erica was stunned. Then she said, "I'll be there as soon as I can make it."

When she went back to the living room they took one look at her face and Louise said, "Bad news."

Erica nodded and told her.

"What can I do?" Steven Kimball said at once. He and Everett were on their feet.

"I've got to get a plane to New York right away and then there are all the Chicago arrangements and . . ." Her voice trailed away; she felt overwhelmed.

"I've got a copter down the road," Steven offered. "I'll fly you right into Houston."

"Oh, I couldn't let you. . . ." Erica began.

"Don't say another word." She was too worried about Merry now to give a thought to this uncomfortable arrangement. But she was very grateful when Louise said, "I'll come with you, too, honey."

"Oh, thank you, thank you!" She hugged Louise, catching a look of exasperation on Everett's face and a disappointed expression on Steven Kimball's.

Everett went to the phone and called the airport.

"You're in luck, honey," he said to Erica when he hung up. "There's a plane at ten and I've got you on it. We can just make it."

Louise handed her the glass of sherry. "You'd better drink the rest of this," she advised. "You look white as a sheet. And sit down, child."

Erica obeyed. "I'll get Maria to pack your things."

Louise summoned the maid, and when the woman had hurried away, she said to Erica, "Now, when you've got your breath, tell me who to notify in Chicago and I'll send telegrams right now."

While Louise was sending the telegrams Erica went up to her room. Her things were packed and one of the boys was already carrying her luggage downstairs. Hastily she smoothed her hair and, without bothering to change, snatched up a bag and ran downstairs to the hall.

Merry could be dying, she thought miserably. And all the way to Houston in the copter, she hardly realized, as Louise soothed her, that her pilot was the man she had resolved to avoid.

All she could think of now was getting to New York, and Merry.

Chapter Eight

$\mathcal{I}$t was nearly four o'clock the next morning before Erica got to the hospital. She had been unable to sleep at all, and the state of feverish impatience she had been in all during the flight and the long drive back to Manhattan had left her feeling shaken and weak.

The nurse outside Intensive Care told her that Merry was resting and could not be seen until that evening.

"Can't I at least take a look at her through the glass?" Erica pleaded.

The nurse shook her head and answered gently, "No, I'm sorry, Miss Warren. I'm under orders."

"Then I need a place to stay here at the hospital," Erica said stubbornly. "Can you get me a cot or something?"

She was aware of the woman's searching scrutiny and thought: I must look like a prospective patient myself.

"Not at the moment, Miss Warren." The nurse hesitated and then suggested, "I really think you should go home and try to get some rest. It won't help your aunt for you to break down, too. And frankly, you look exhausted. I understand you've just flown into town."

"Yes." Reluctantly Erica accepted the wisdom of the suggestion. "You're right," she admitted. "I'm dead tired. What time can I see her this evening?"

"About seven. Please, Miss Warren," the woman said. "Dr. Grant has your number, of course, and you'll be notified immediately if there's any change."

"All right." Erica suddenly felt dizzy with tiredness and defeated by the nurse's gentle calm. "All right. Thank you."

Unwilling to wake the servants at the town house, Erica telephoned for a cab. Seeing her look of exhaustion the sympathetic driver put her overnight case in the cab and even helped her in—a phenomenon, she thought with weary humor, for a New York cabbie. She was glad she'd had the presence of mind to check her luggage at the airport for someone to pick up later.

The city was still in darkness as the taxi whirred down Fifth Avenue, the black mass of Central Park like a gloomy forest full of sinister things. Erica shivered; she had been too upset to unpack a coat and her light suit was insufficient for the cold late-autumn air. Her nerves stretched taut. What if Merry should die? she thought with pain.

She let herself quietly into the house and, setting down her overnight case in the hall, went into the living room to turn on some lights and relax a moment before going upstairs. She still felt wide-awake, in spite of her deep exhaustion.

Snapping on a lamp by the door she stopped on the threshold, astonished. The living room was a perfect garden—no, more than that, an absolute sea of flowers. They covered practically every surface: tables, mantelpiece, piano. There were even large vases of them at either end of the hearth and other points throughout the room.

Erica had never seen so many flowers: hundreds of roses—red, pink, coral, yellow and white; anemones and lilies; birds of paradise and carnations. It was an incredible display.

Preoccupied with this new sight, so much so that she momentarily forgot to be anxious, Erica sank down on the couch and looked around. Where on earth had they all come from?

Then she remembered that flowers were not allowed in Intensive Care. All these must be for Merry. Erica hadn't realized she had so many friends.

But why had Hattie put them all in here? The

poor thing, Erica reflected, must have become totally unnerved by Merry's sudden illness. She looked around for cards, expecting to see a pile of them on the table where such things were sometimes left.

But there was only one. A plain white card addressed to Miss Erica Warren, with no greeting, no signature.

"Oh . . ." Erica whispered aloud. It seemed inconceivable that one person could have sent all these. She went out into the hall to see if there were cards on the hall table. There were none, but here also there were masses of flowers.

Erica shook her head, picked up her overnight case and went upstairs. On tables in the hall were still more flowers. When she opened the door to her room there were even more.

It was too mysterious to understand; surely Morgan wouldn't . . . No. Erica shook her head. This wasn't Morgan's style at all, even if he had the means.

The means . . . Only one man she knew could even afford to do this. Steven Kimball.

Still puzzling it out, Erica undressed hurriedly and showered. Feeling the stinging, grateful warmth of the shower on her hair and face and body, she repeated silently: Steven Kimball.

Moving like a sleepwalker, Erica toweled herself dry and went into the bedroom. She screwed up enough energy to blow-dry her hair and without even putting on a nightgown collapsed under the turned-down cover.

Her last waking thought was: What an incredible thing. Whoever had sent the absurd, extravagant mass of flowers had accomplished what no one else could. He had kept her mind off Merry for almost half an hour.

Erica slept deeply for nine hours, waking at two in the afternoon with a guilty start. Still only half-alert, she picked up the phone by her bed and dialed the hospital. She spoke to Dr. Grant. There was little change in Merry; she was still unconscious. The doctor advised Erica to check again in two hours, but she decided to go to the hospital herself and wait there.

There was a light tap at the door and Hattie stuck her grizzled head around the doorframe. "Miss Erica!" Her kindly, weathered face was all smiles, but Erica could see the effects of her recent anxiety. Her plump cheeks sagged and there were dark circles below her eyes. "Welcome home." She came in with a tray holding coffee and toast.

"Oh, thank you, Hattie." Erica smiled at the old woman. "This is so sweet of you." She never had breakfast in bed unless she was ill; in fact, she positively disliked it, but she didn't want to hurt Hattie's feelings.

"I heard you coming in this morning," Hattie said. "You must have been all tuckered out."

"I was. But I'm much better now." Erica took a sip of coffee; it tasted wonderful. "I was calling the hospital just now," she said. "There's no change. I'll be going there later. You feel free to come as often as you like, too, although I don't know what good any of us can do her right now."

Her grim tone was echoed in Hattie's voice

when the latter replied, "I know. I appreciate that, Miss Erica. But I guess I'll just stay here and hold the fort for you right now, at least until . . ." She stopped, looking stricken. They both knew what was in her mind.

As much to distract herself as Hattie from their gloomy thoughts Erica asked quickly, "Now what about all these flowers? I couldn't find the cards anywhere. I've never seen so many in my life."

Hattie looked relieved and pleased, as if the strange happening were a very welcome topic. "There was only the one card," she declared. "I couldn't believe my eyes, Miss Erica. It was nearly midnight and we were all about asleep when the doorbell rang. I was that frightened," she confided. "Didn't know who it could be at that hour; I knew if it was the hospital they would've called. And you couldn't have gotten here that fast. When Mrs. Kerr called me last night she said you wouldn't even be leaving Texas until ten or so, their time . . ." she rattled on.

"But what happened?" Erica prompted gently.

"Well, I went to the door and there was this man saying he had a delivery for Miss Warren. I said, 'A likely story. You get away from this door or I'll call the police.' I still had the chain on, you see. And he said, 'Look here, lady, it's flowers. The guy who sent them got my boss out of bed and *he* got *us* out of bed. Of course, we're getting premium pay.' Then he grinned and he said, 'Look.' I looked out and there was a big truck with the florist's name on it. I was still afraid they were burglars and it was some kind of trick. So I says, 'Well, you just bring the flowers out, then, and leave 'em on the stoop.'

"And he says, 'Lady, you'll be sorry. You never seen so many flowers in your life.' And he was right. They began to pile up on the stoop. So I thought: Well, if these are burglars they sure spent a mint to play their trick and it didn't make sense they were going to rob us. But all those flowers, at midnight. I ask you, Miss Erica!"

Hattie made a comical face and for the first time in days Erica laughed aloud. I'm really home, she thought. Hattie's urban caution was so typical of New York residents.

"So they kept bringing them and bringing them," Hattie went on, "and I got James up to help me. I must say, whoever it was was mighty considerate. Most of the flowers were already in vases and they even had water in them! Even so it took us awhile to get them all arranged. I'd've hated for the pretty things to die. The florist's men helped, too. Finally I said, 'Well, you've brought a wagonload of flowers. Where's the cards?' And the fellow says, 'This is it,' and handed me the card. No name on it at all but yours. Who do *you* think sent them, Miss Erica?"

"I can't imagine," Erica lied. But something must have shown on her face because Hattie studied her and a ghost of a smile played around her mouth.

"Well," she remarked, "if it's a beau, he's mighty serious. It was a grand thing to do. Got my mind right off Miss Merry last night *and* just now."

"And mine, too." Erica smiled. Then she sobered. "I'd better be getting to the hospital soon. Could you please send James to the airport to get my luggage? The claim tickets are on my dresser."

"I'll see to it right now. When Miss Merry's out of that Intensive Care, will you be wanting some of these flowers sent to her at the hospital?"

"Oh, yes, Hattie. Thank you for thinking of it. *Most* of them, as a matter of fact. I'm sure the other patients in the hospital will appreciate them. Do that . . . when she's in a regular room again."

Hattie's optimistic suggestion had heartened Erica. When she got to the hospital she felt far different from the way she had the visit before. Strengthened by food and rest, refreshed by a change of clothes, she felt able to cope better now with whatever came.

Dr. Grant met her outside Intensive Care. "She's conscious," he said. But his cautious look belied the good news.

"What is it?" Erica asked anxiously. "Will she be all right? Why are you looking like that?" The questions tumbled out.

"Please, my dear." Dr. Grant smiled tiredly and put his hand on her shoulder. "I'm going to let you go in for a moment or two. But first we'd better talk. Sit down."

He led her to one of the soft waiting-room chairs. Unwillingly she sat down on the edge of it, waiting.

"What is it?" she asked impatiently. "Please don't mince your words, Dr. Grant. I want to know."

"Very well." He looked serious. "She's going to be all right, yes. But she's paralyzed on one side," he concluded bluntly. "She can't talk."

Erica's heart was in her mouth; she felt her skin turn cold. "Paralyzed?" she repeated in a whisper.

Dr. Grant nodded. "It may be quite awhile before she's herself again. I just wanted to prepare you, Erica. It's not an easy thing, seeing an active woman like Meredith in this condition."

"But . . . how long will this go on?" she demanded.

"I have no way of knowing. I just can't tell you. I'm sorry; I wish I could, my dear. Do you want to go in now?"

"Oh, yes. Yes, of course." Erica followed the doctor into Merry's room and was stricken with grief to see the terrible change in the vital, intelligent woman. She hoped her thoughts hadn't shown on her face; she tried to smile as she went toward the bed.

"Hello," she said in a soft voice, bending to kiss Merry's cheek. When she straightened, looking down at her helpless aunt, it was shocking to contemplate her.

Merry's handsome mouth was askew, drawn to one side of her face, and the grimace had even affected one of her eyes, which sagged at the corner, looking sad while the other one was intelligent and alert.

But Erica kept smiling and said, "I'm so glad you're better."

Merry's answering attempt at a smile was such a travesty that Erica nearly burst into tears. But she controlled herself sternly. Thank heavens, at least, there was no brain damage, she told herself. Merry's clear intelligence shone like a beacon through her distorted features.

Merry made a slight motion with her unaffected hand; Erica was heartened to notice that it was her right hand. It would still be possible for her to write notes, then, even if she couldn't talk yet.

Merry made the gesture again. Understanding at once, Erica took a small pad and pen from her handbag and passed them to Merry.

Laboriously the older woman began to form big scrawling block letters in a brief message: "DONT . . . LOSE . . . WARREN."

Erica read the message and stared, amazed, at Merry. She read it again and, looking at Merry, nodded solemnly.

"I won't," she whispered. "I promise you." She noticed that the nurse was hovering impatiently near and looked significantly at Dr. Grant. He moved toward the bed.

"Erica . . ." he began warningly.

But now Merry was obviously annoyed, for she made an almost peremptory gesture with her undamaged right hand and something like a frown creased her brow. Erica was gladdened to see that; no one who was mortally ill could show that much vitality.

Her aunt gestured to Erica for the pen. Erica put it in her fingers again and, leaning over, watched her print: "GET . . . GATES . . . HERE . . . WATCH . . . GEORGE."

"Get Gates here. Watch George," Erica repeated. Her aunt wanted her lawyer to come to the hospital. And Erica was to "watch George." He was up to something, then.

"Yes. Yes, I'll do both," she said in a firm voice to Merry Blaine. Erica bent to kiss her, then left the room.

"That's an *extremely* good sign," Dr. Grant said a few minutes later. "We feared brain damage, but as you can see there is none at all. The fact that she can reason and communicate with you is evidence that she still has all her faculties. It seems to me that she'll recover sooner than I thought."

Erica's heart was thudding in her breast; she felt weak with joyful relief. "Oh, I'm so glad, so glad," she kept repeating.

"Well, my dear, things are looking up," Dr. Grant said, pressing Erica's arm. "But I'm afraid I'll have to bar you now until tomorrow. Once a day is enough for the time being."

"I don't know whether you saw the content of her last note . . ." Erica began. Dr. Grant shook his head. "She urgently wants to see her lawyer," she went on. "I hope you will allow that, because I think it's important to her."

"Well, yes, I think I can. Provided, of course,

that a nurse and I are always present. We must be present, naturally, during all visits."

"Certainly. Then may I arrange for him to come tomorrow?"

"Yes," Dr. Grant said. "Early evening. Not before."

"All right. I'll arrange it."

Erica left the hospital with new hope in her heart. One of the things she'd have to do tonight, she resolved, was to talk to Jenny.

Paul came back to the bedroom with a resentful look and turned down the volume of the television. "It's the queen bee. For you. At"—he glared at his watch—"nine-thirty at night."

"Oh, Paul," Jenny said resignedly. She got out of bed and padded barefoot into the living room. "Erica," she said eagerly into the phone.

"Oh, Jenny, I'm sorry to bother you at this hour." Erica sounded tired and pressed.

"It's okay," Jenny assured her. "How is Mrs. Blaine? I wanted to go to the hospital, but of course they wouldn't allow any visitors, not even flowers, so . . ." She paused and asked, "How are *you*?"

"Tired, but catching up. Merry's better, thank God. No brain damage. She even wrote me notes."

"That's wonderful." Jenny waited, feeling Paul's disapproving presence in the other room. The television volume was still turned almost too low to hear, in a martyred way, as if in reproach.

"I would have called you during office hours," Erica went on, "but I was asleep almost all day."

"Really, it's all right." Jenny looked up. Paul was standing in the doorway to the bedroom, staring at her, a sarcastic, nasty expression on his face. Jenny turned away and asked into the phone, "Anything I can do?"

"I just wanted to get a general idea of what's going on," Erica said apologetically. "I know I've been hard to keep up with these last few days, changing my schedule right and left. Is there anything special?"

"Fortunately, nothing urgent or disastrous. There is one thing, though, but I didn't want to put it into writing. I'd like to talk to you about it. It's the darndest thing. . . . I don't quite know how to tell you."

"George." Erica's guess was immediate. Jenny was surprised. "It's about George Blaine," Erica repeated.

"Why, yes. But how in the world did you know? I think I'm working for a witch, not a tycoon." Jenny giggled. Paul turned away with a snort of disgust and disappeared into the bedroom.

"I'll tell you about it tomorrow. Now, what was it about George?"

Jenny told her.

"I see." Erica's voice was noncommittal, but Jenny thought she heard a note of triumph in it. "Well, thank you. See you in the morning. Regards to Paul."

"Right. See you bright and early." Jenny hung

up and, reluctant to face Paul, went into the kitchen for a glass of milk. She sat down at the table to drink it.

"Well, well." She looked up, startled. She hadn't heard him approaching. "So you're still snapping to when Her Highness calls."

Jenny tried to suppress her rising irritation. Paul had that spoiling-for-a-fight air that she dreaded. She was determined not to fall into the trap again. "She couldn't call today," Jenny explained patiently. "I'm sorry if it disturbs you. But she was asleep."

"*Asleep?*" Paul snorted and went to the refrigerator. He took out a beer and slammed the door hard. Flipping the can open, he took a swallow and repeated, "Asleep. All day, I suppose, while the peasants were slaving in the fields for her royal profit."

"Oh, for heaven's sake, Paul." Jenny was really mad now and could no longer contain her anger. "Don't give me all that nineteenth-century nonsense. You sound like a bad Russian novel. She flew back from Texas late last night and hadn't slept at all, I'm sure. Why shouldn't she sleep today?"

"You know, the way you defend her is ridiculous. It was great when she was gone. You paid some attention to me; it was almost like the early days."

"You mean I had a few more hours each night to wear myself out spoiling you rotten when about all you do during the week is go to school and leave everything else to me." Jenny stopped, appalled that she had said so much and said it so nastily. But all the things she'd been suppressing had suddenly come out.

"How many more times are you going to rub my nose in the fact that I'm a no-good kept bum?"

Jenny realized that the argument was going too far; she wanted desperately to smooth things over, to regain some of the hard-won peace they'd enjoyed during the last week or so.

"I'm sorry, Paul . . . really I am," she said quietly. "But you've got to admit that it's a bit difficult"—she fought to keep her words restrained—"taking care of so many things at once: the job, the house, our clothes and the cooking and all the other stuff. . . ." Her voice trailed off into weary silence.

But what she'd said hadn't appeased him. He said in a loud, angry voice, "It looks like you really fouled up, then. You shouldn't have married me in the first place. Maybe you should have waited until the queen bee could pick out somebody from her set." He took another swallow of beer.

"It seems to me you've had enough of those already," Jenny couldn't help saying, even though she had wanted to smooth things over, to make up.

"And don't start on *that*," he shouted. "Maybe I need it to get me through this farce—this farce of a school, where I'll learn to be a hack . . . this farce of a marriage." He finished the beer while she sat in miserable silence, staring at him with tears in her eyes. Putting the empty beer can on the table, he stormed out of the kitchen and went back in the bedroom. She heard the door slam and the television volume turned up loud.

With a kind of grieving resentment Jenny picked up the empty can and put it in the garbage. Then she rinsed her glass and went into the living room. She decided stubbornly to sleep on the couch. Paul didn't emerge from the bedroom to seek her out and as she drifted into lonely sleep she thought: Maybe the job is all I have. And maybe this marriage is a farce that should be ended for both our sakes. When she woke up the next morning Paul had already left the house. More than ever Jenny looked forward to her day at Warren's, where she was really needed—and understood.

In one swift moment she realized that the only time she was really happy these days was when she was on the job. It was a desolate conclusion but she couldn't avoid it any longer. There was only one sensible thing to do.

While she drank her coffee she wrote a note and left it on the kitchen table. Then she took a big suitcase off a closet shelf and began to pack.

Erica was already in her office when Jenny arrived. She could hardly help noticing the big suitcase her assistant was struggling with. Blushing, Jenny called out a warm good morning and quickly stowed the case behind a filing cabinet, as if it were a guilty secret. Even in her preoccupation with all the work that awaited her and her anxiety over Merry, Erica felt a compassionate concern for the blond girl. It was all too obvious, from her slightly red-rimmed eyes and her woebegone look, what the suitcase meant.

"Jenny. Come in here a moment, will you?"

"Of course. Shall I bring my book?"

"Not right now." When Jenny had come in Erica shut the door and sat down behind her desk. "Sit," she urged casually, smiling. "Let's talk."

"Is everything all right?" Jenny asked anxiously. "I . . . I figured I had things pretty well squared away, and there's no new—"

"Jenny," Erica cut in softly. "It's not the work, honey. Everything's in fantastic shape. You did a great job while I was away. In fact"—her smile widened—"you almost make me feel superfluous with the way you handled some things, but we'll get to all that in time. Why the suitcase?" she demanded bluntly.

"I guess you should know. I've left Paul." Erica studied her assistant; Jenny looked more stubborn and determined than sad at the moment and Erica considered it a good sign.

"I see," she said neutrally. "Where are you staying?"

"Nowhere yet. I'll probably check into a hotel for the time being." Jenny's woebegone look had returned.

"Why not stay with me at the house?" Erica suggested lightly. "I think you'll find the guest room comfortable . . . and you'd be doing me a favor. It's pretty lonely without my aunt."

"Oh, Erica." Jenny studied her. "Are you sure?

You don't fool me about being lonely; I think you're just being nice, as usual."

"I really *am* lonely there right now," Erica assured her. "If you'd like to stay you're welcome."

"I'd love it. Thank you."

"Okay. Enough of that for the moment. We'll talk some more tonight. Now I'd better get to work," Erica said.

The first order of business, she decided after Jenny had left, was a conference with Harold Gates, Merry's attorney. She dialed his office herself, making an appointment for two that afternoon. She wanted to fill him in on Merry's condition and also check a few things out. She had an uneasy feeling that George might be up to something in regard to Merry's stocks.

She concentrated for the next few hours on her work and made an appointment for a conference with the corporation's chief attorney to discuss Kimren matters and catch up with the legal aspects of Warren stock transactions. Then she called her broker and made a date with him before heading out to lunch.

It was ten after five when she got back to the office. Her head ached and she felt apprehensive and tired. None of the conferences had been very satisfactory. The chief attorney had warned her that Kimco now held a small but dangerous percentage of common stock; Gates had advised her that George Blaine had already been to see him, making the outrageous suggestion that Meredith Blaine be declared *non compos mentis* because of her stroke and asking for her power of attorney. Gates had assured Erica that he felt, after a long conversation with Merry's physician, that her mind was anything but unsound and that her power of attorney would be likely to rest with Erica in view of the clear terms of Josh Warren's will, but that George could still be "a nuisance."

Erica's broker reported something even stranger and more disturbing: George Blaine had sold two percent of his stock to Kimco. From that she could draw a gloomy pair of conclusions—George was desperate for money and he was so hostile toward her now that he would rather see an outside company take control than let it stay in her hands.

Jenny was sitting at her desk reading a magazine when Erica came in.

"Oh, oh." Jenny looked at her sharply. "It didn't go well."

"You've got that right," Erica answered tiredly. "Let's get out of here. I'll take you to the house. We can have an early dinner; I have to get over to the hospital by seven."

Jenny assented gladly. At the town house Erica explained to Hattie that Mrs. Landon would be their guest for a while. She was touched to see how the motherly housekeeper took Jenny under her wing and was also gratified by Jenny's pleasure in the room, the dinner and everything about the Warren house. Somehow this made up for the disturbing conferences of the afternoon.

As she drove to the hospital Erica reflected on

how much she had missed by never having brothers or sisters. Maybe Jenny would help make up for that too, she thought.

She was encouraged by Merry's bright-eyed look and the slight improvement in her distorted face when Dr. Grant allowed her to look in briefly. "If she keeps this up," the doctor said, smiling, "we'll have her in a regular room in a couple of days."

Erica waited in the outside room while Harold Gates went in to see Merry. He emerged with a look of satisfaction. "Your aunt," he said, "has indicated to me in writing that you should have her power of attorney."

"Well, well. My timing is perfect." Erica wheeled around and saw George Blaine at the door of the waiting room. He was smiling his unpleasant smile, but his eyes were hard with hatred.

"This isn't the last of it, Mr. Gates," he said to the lawyer. "You'll hear from my lawyer in the morning." He turned on his heel and walked out.

Gates shook his head. "He doesn't have a prayer," he said to Erica. "But as I said before, he'll have plenty of nuisance value." He stared at Erica. "You know, it's appalling, my dear; he didn't even ask how his mother was feeling." He clasped her hand and left.

How right you are, Mr. Gates, Erica thought. And where, for that matter, was Roger? More than ever she admired the sagacity of her grandfather. Josh Warren had known what he was doing, all right, with that outrageous provision in his will.

Erica went downstairs, her spirits rising. Dr. Grant had said that she could see Merry twice tomorrow and that, very likely, the next day she'd be moved to a regular room.

The lights along Fifth Avenue and the gold-white headlights of passing taxis and cars had never looked so festive or beautiful as they did to Erica when she emerged into the crisply cold night air.

She headed toward her car. A tall man stepped out of the shadows, saying with great casualness, "Hello again, Erica. How's Mrs. Blaine?"

Erica recognized the deep growling voice at once, even before the lights revealed the man's face.

It was Steven Kimball.

Chapter Nine

Those commanding silver eyes of his blazed at her in the passing traffic lights like those of a wildcat. And his leanness, his close-fitting dark clothes and his lithe cautious stance also reminded her of a panther. Blast him, she thought, his magnetism never lessened; he always put her at a disadvantage in their encounters.

She remembered the flowers, and something soft and laughing bloomed in her in spite of herself. In that moment she was at an utter loss. But then, determined not to let him see how strongly he affected her, she answered quietly, "Much better."

"I'm glad." They stood there staring at each other and to break the awkward pause she said, "I want to thank you for being so kind and . . . helpful in Texas. And for the flowers."

He shrugged his massive shoulders. "That was nothing." Then he demanded abruptly, "Do you have your aunt's power of attorney, Erica?"

Suddenly she turned cold. "Why do you ask that?"

"Please." He took a step toward her, touching her arm. "Don't be so suspicious. Just answer me."

It came to her, then, why he was really there. All he had wanted to know was that—where the power of attorney lay now. And wasn't it just a little too coincidental that he should show up here tonight?

"Erica, why don't you let me take you somewhere quiet where we can talk? We can't stand here discussing these matters on the street."

Why not? she decided. It would be interesting to see what he had to say, to find out just how far his game had gone.

"All right," she said neutrally. "My car's right here."

When they got in he made a slight move toward her and then settled back. She knew her expression was cold and far from encouraging.

"The Palm Court?"

She nodded and drove off down Fifth Avenue. Neither of them spoke during the drive downtown. She turned into the oval before the gracious Plaza Hotel; an attendant came to open the door for her and to park the car.

Still silent, she led the way into the beautiful Palm Court and they were shown to a secluded table half obscured by the tall green fronds of the potted trees; a string quartet was playing softly.

Steven consulted her about her choice of drinks, gave the order and leaned toward her as the waiter went away.

"It seems a shame," she said with sudden bitterness, "to keep your spy waiting." She'd meant to go slow; it had just slipped out.

"My spy?" He looked bewildered. "Who do you mean?"

The waiter was returning with their cocktails. Erica paused until he had set them down and moved off, then snapped, "George Blaine. He's one of your sources of information, I think?"

"Of course he is," Steven said roughly. "But you don't understand this thing. You don't understand it at all."

"I understand all I need to." She took a sip of her drink and looked away.

"Please, Erica." Steven Kimball reached across the marble table and took her hand. His touch, as it always did, set off a wild, hot longing in her hungry body. The point of heat that began where his strong fingers touched her swept up her arm to her shoulder, to the drumming pulse below her ear. She thought: Damn him, damn him. Why am I so helpless when he touches me?

"You've got to let me explain it."

"How can you explain?" she demanded.

"Surely you must know that Blaine and Hunt are—"

"So it's Morgan now, too, is it?" she said angrily. "You're jealous of him—you've always been jealous—so you want to involve him in your maneuvers with George. For your information I know that George hates me enough to help you take over Warren's, even if he loses. But I doubt he'll lose in the transaction. I'm sure you'll see to that."

"Erica, it's Hunt who began it all," Steven said firmly.

"I don't believe you. You're implying that no one can love me for myself, only for my money." She was furious, resentful and deeply hurt.

"Don't be ridiculous," he said in a savage tone. "Do you think Miami happened because of money?"

"Yes." She could feel the tears gathering in her eyes and, exasperated, blinked them away. "It was all part of your great master plan. You've been using me. It's some kind of joke with you—trying to take over my company and making love to me on the side, like a kind of . . . kind of fringe benefit," she concluded angrily. "Although I'm sure that 'love' was the last thing on your mind." The hot words tumbled out.

She snatched her hand away and he did not try to reclaim it. He shook his dark head.

"For a bright girl, you sound . . ." He stopped. "Never mind."

"Why did you ask me about my aunt's power of attorney?" she insisted.

"Because I wanted to know. Because it's important." His voice sounded weary, almost indifferent now.

"Important to *you*, you mean."

He sighed. "Never mind, Erica. I won't be bothering you again. I'm going to Europe tomorrow. On a long trip. And after that, to Japan." He raised his hand and signaled to the waiter. "Another?" he asked her.

She shook her head. As he gave the waiter an order for another bourbon she realized that she felt strangely desolate. He sounded so different all of a sudden—disinterested, remote. And when the waiter brought his drink he drank it quickly before asking for the check. She had wanted desperately to hear more of what he had to say, but like a rash fool she'd blurted out all kinds of things and caused him to withdraw. And now it was too late.

Yet some devil in her prompted her to retort, "You'll still be in touch with your brokers, though, I take it. Just remember this, I'm on to you now. And I'll also be in touch with mine."

His face stiffened but his bright eyes were unreadable. He smiled in an ironic way and commented, "That's all you really care about, isn't it, Erica? It's all you've ever cared about— your position of power. You were right, lady. We *are* two of a kind. And you're right about my brokers. I'll be in close touch with them; it'll be a pleasure."

He paid the check and asked her coolly, "May I see you to your car?"

She nodded, miserable, hardly knowing whether what she felt was pain or anger. But of one thing she was sure: She was more confused than ever.

They stood in formal silence on the steps of the lovely old hotel, waiting for the attendant to deliver Erica's car. When it arrived Steven tipped the man and handed her in himself.

Out of politeness she started to ask him if she could drop him anywhere, then realized how awkward and foolish that would be. He seemed to recognize her small dilemma, for he smiled satirically as he leaned into the window.

"Good night, Ice Princess. Run along home now and go to bed with your forty-nine percent."

Without another word he straightened and walked off; she saw him heading uptown on Fifth Avenue. Exasperated, she started her car and drove east.

She was trembling so much that she was hard put to drive, but she got herself sternly in control and slowed down. What kind of a man was he? she asked herself as she pulled into the porte cochere of the town house and into the garage. What kind of a game was he really playing?

She felt drained as she went into the house and up the stairs. She could hear the television set playing softly in the guest room. It wasn't even nine o'clock, yet she was exhausted.

She entered her room and closed the door. Stripping off her clothes and hanging them up, she padded to the bathroom and ran the water for a long, luxurious bath. Her nerves were in knots and she needed desperately to relax.

Pouring her carnation bubble bath into the steaming water she thought of Steven and the afternoon of their encounter at the harbor and how the caress of the bath that night had reminded her of the touch of a man's hands. Lying back in the foaming bubbles she realized that it was the same tonight.

But it was worse this time. Worse than it had ever been. For now she also had the memory of their wild, abandoned night of love. Now she intimately knew Steven's body and he knew hers. But every time they had met it had been like a kind of duel.

She finished bathing, dried and wandered back to her room, still deeply weary but wide-awake. After getting into a nightgown she chose a book from the shelves and got into bed.

She remembered his scornful direction: "Go to bed with your forty-nine percent."

Erica threw down the book. With a sinking heart she knew that, whatever he had done, she wanted him. And she loved him. Now that he was going off for heaven knew how long she realized that he was the one man she had always waited for.

But he was trying to hurt her, another part of her mind argued; he was trying to take over Warren's. Angrily she picked up the book again and tried to concentrate on it. Yet the dilemma intruded, making it almost impossible for her to read.

When she finally gave up, utter tiredness driving her to a restless sleep, the problem nagged at her still. Steven Kimball came to her in her uneasy dreams.

* * *

The next morning, however, Erica woke refreshed and renewed, determined to put him out of her mind for good—at least, Steven Kimball the man. But Kimball the competitor was someone to keep in her sights at all times, she decided. She would not let him take any more than he had already; she was determined about that.

In the days that followed Erica had so much to occupy her that she barely had time to think of anything personal and she blessed that fact. Merry was so improved that Dr. Grant predicted she'd be at home within a couple of weeks; the bright, determined old lady was working like a beaver at her exercises and the doctor declared her a miracle.

"She'll be walking before we turn around," he told Erica, his eyes twinkling. "With the aid of a cane, of course."

Erica began to feel a restless yearning to complete her interrupted tour. On a visit to Merry, who now was able to speak in a slow, rather slurred manner, she wasn't surprised when her aunt drawled, "How long are you going to waste your time?"

"What do you mean?"

"With me." Merry, unable to waste words these days, was more telegraphic than ever. "Get on that trip."

"But I don't want to leave you," Erica protested, taking Merry's hand.

"Pooh." The sound, in Merry's stiff, awkward mouth, was comical. "I go home Thursday."

Erica admitted that she wanted to be off

again. Even though Kimball had threatened to be in touch with his brokers there had been no new activity in Warren stock trading.

Finally she decided to travel between Thanksgiving and Christmas. She wanted to spend the holidays with Merry and with Jenny.

The "couple of days" of Jenny's visit had extended into weeks. Erica was insistent that the girl stay on in the town house because now she felt a protective interest in her that went beyond their friendship. Jenny worked with her usual zest and responded with delight to the luxury of the house in her leisure hours; yet she didn't seem happy. Erica knew she missed Paul. What the contact between them had been she didn't know, because Jenny had become totally reticent on the matter and Erica didn't like to pry. But she could see that Jenny had lost weight and sometimes gave evidence of having cried during the night when she came down in the morning.

The media were again in pursuit of Steven Kimball. He had obviously reverted to his secretive way of life, because Erica read almost nothing of him these days. He had once more become Mr. Mask, she thought bitterly, thankful that she had seen behind that mask. She'd been right all along: He hadn't changed at all. Erica Warren had only been challenging prey for a spoiled playboy. Her heart ached when she thought that and something in her protested, but she was more than ever determined not to listen to that faint protest.

The only hints Erica received of his activities were from the financial papers: The Europe trip was related to Kimren and his upcoming Japanese tour to Sonakim, Kimball's huge electronic subsidiary.

She was on the plane to Chicago when she caught sight of his name in a gossip column: "Irrepressible Arabella Loving is making *vita* more *dolce* these days for Steven (Mr. Mask) Kimball. They're a frequent duo in smart spots around the Eternal City."

Erica threw the newspaper on the empty seat beside her, hardly knowing whether to laugh or cry. Arabella again. That *is* his style, she reflected gloomily. And she made still another resolution to put him completely out of mind.

She was successful in doing so for a few days, but when she flew to Detroit she saw his name coupled with Arabella's again in still another column, this time with the information that he would be touring Japan after the new year. Erica realized that she would be on the Coast then, easy flying distance from Japan. Annoyed to find herself thinking like that, she threw herself into the midwestern project with even greater energy and began to plan for Christmas in New York.

Back in New York Erica kept herself almost frenetically active as the holiday approached. Merry still wasn't up to her usual activities, although she was now walking slowly, as Dr. Grant had predicted, with a cane. A temporary bedroom had been set up for her on the first floor of the town house since the winding stairs couldn't accommodate an elevated chair to get her up and down.

Erica rushed home from the office each afternoon to supervise the decoration of the house so that Merry would not tire herself too much, and she shopped far and wide for special presents for Merry, Jenny and a few friends. George was markedly absent from their lives, although Erica ran into Morgan at several holiday parties.

She was in good spirits about business, but really worried now about Jenny. She had gotten so thin it had been necessary to have her clothes altered so they wouldn't hang on her. She was more secretive than ever and, although she was functioning at work with the same efficiency, Erica thought sadly that now it was just that— functioning. She no longer worked with the eagerness and zeal she had always shown before.

Jenny seemed to have no social life whatsoever; she came home after work, smiled politely through dinner, then shut herself up in her room. She was warmly grateful for Erica's presents at Christmas but refused to enter into any of the other festivities, saying that she was tired when people arrived for the Warren's Christmas party.

Erica suspected that Paul had telephoned her on Christmas Eve, but knew nothing beyond that. She wondered what kind of man he was to let things go this long. She'd expected him to turn up at the house weeks ago.

Some of the mystery was solved on the afternoon of December 31, the same afternoon that Erica and Merry had a spirited debate on the subject of New Year's Eve.

Erica was in the living room with her aunt.

The indomitable Merry, whose speech was now practically restored, seemed almost her old self. She had been sitting by the fire, reading, when Erica had wandered in.

"What's the matter with you, child?" Merry had demanded. She put her open book on her lap and stared at her niece. "You don't know what to do with yourself today. Quit prowling around and sit down. Talk to me."

Trying to avoid her aunt's sharp eyes, Erica sat down on the couch.

"Not there," Merry said sharply. "Here. I want to take a good look at you." She patted the arm of the chair next to hers.

Feeling like a small disobedient child, Erica said, "I'm fine here."

"All right." Merry sounded resigned. "You can avoid me, my dear, but you can't go on avoiding the thing that's bothering you, any more than Jenny can. Both of you make me tired. What's wrong with that girl? I'm very fond of her, but she never says a word to me about anything. She and that awful boy should either fish or cut bait. Are they going to get a divorce or go on like this forever? And as for you, miss, you're even worse. Are you going to sit here in the house tonight or go out like other people?"

Erica couldn't help smiling. "You know, if you weren't bugging me so much I'd be delighted to hear you sound like this. You're almost as cantankerous as you were before you got sick. I think you're well again."

"Don't change the subject," Merry snapped,

but her sharp tone didn't fool Erica; she could see the real concern in her aunt's lively gray eyes. "Erica, my dear," Merry said more softly, "you know how I feel about women's independence. I've told you time and again that I admire you for what you're doing. And I think Jenny ought to have a medal for putting up with that ne'er-do-well for so long. But my dear, there *is* more to life than your work." She smiled.

"As big a scoundrel as your uncle was, I loved him. . . . And when I was your age I had two sons already. Yet here you both are, two beautiful young women planning to spend New Year's Eve alone with an old useless woman." Merry put out her hand and gestured to Erica. "Please come sit here."

Erica obeyed and Merry patted her arm.

"Now what is it all about?" Merry asked. "Hattie told me about the flower incident." She chuckled. "I must say, I admire any man with enough imagination to do such an extravagant thing. Who sent them . . . ? The man you've been brooding about?"

"Yes," Erica admitted. Embarrassed, she longed for an escape from the subject. She heard the phone ring in the hall. Quickly she got up. "I'll get it."

"Sit down, child. You know Hattie will answer. Are you expecting a call?"

"Not really."

Merry made an exasperated sound. "I never know what that namby-pamby answer means."

Erica heard Hattie's voice. Then she listened

as Hattie called up the stairs, "It's for you, Miss Jenny."

Erica, feeling an irrational childish disappointment, thought: Why doesn't he call me? Mercifully her aunt made no further comment as Erica got up and wandered to the window.

In an amazingly short time Jenny rushed into the room. Her face was transfigured.

"Good news?" Erica asked, smiling.

"Yes." Jenny's blue eyes were shining.

"Well, tell us about it, child!" Merry scolded, although her eyes were kindly.

Jenny plumped herself down on the couch and said softly, "That was Paul."

Erica retorted teasingly, *"Really?"*

"He's been upstate, visiting his parents, during the holidays. But he's back in town now. And we're going out tonight." She looked shyly at Merry and Erica, then went on. "Everything has changed. Everything. He sounds . . . totally different. He says he sees everything in a different light now, that . . . that he's been . . . a fool. After he graduates he's taking a marvelous job."

"That's wonderful," Erica said warmly. She went over to Jenny and kissed her on the cheek.

"Well, it's about time he came to his senses," Merry said tartly. But it was clear that she was very happy for the younger girl.

Paul appeared that night about eight and Erica had never seen him look so trim and confident. He had had his hair trimmed and he wore a neat sports jacket and flannel trousers under his overcoat. Even, she marveled, a tie.

Erica was delighted for Jenny; she had never looked so beautiful.

But later, when she was seeing the New Year in with Merry, Erica felt very sorry for herself. I was right not to take him seriously, she thought. Only a man who didn't care could forget the holidays, when it seemed that the whole world was paired off in twos.

A few days later, as her plane was coming into San Francisco, Erica felt more like herself. Her gloom had evaporated in her eagerness to see again the charming city of flowers and hills, of mists and wharves, the splendor of the matchless Golden Gate. Those who lost their hearts to San Francisco, she thought, did so for good reason, because it had everything—an ideal location, a picturesque topography, a springlike climate and warm, open people.

As she was disembarking the smiling stewardess wished her a pleasant stay, revealing that the temperature was fifty-four today in San Francisco. As often as she had been here, Erica was always amazed at the mildness of a San Francisco winter. Now a gentle drizzle began to fall, making a silver shine of the air.

While her taxi turned onto the Embarcadero Freeway, past the long Bay Bridge, and pulled up before the dramatic Hyatt Regency Erica's pleasure grew. The hotel was a striking heptagon towering triangularly eighteen stories over the Embarcadero Fountain. She stepped into the startling lobby, a light-filled atrium eighteen stories tall with crystal bubble elevators gliding up and down in majestic splendor. Flowers bloomed by the hundreds and exotic birds sang; there were babbling brooks and more than a hundred trees. Erica looked up with delight at the golden sculpture *Eclipse,* a hollow sphere that was a triumph of constructivist art.

After registering she ascended in one of the shining glass elevators to her suite. The trip had hardly tired her at all, so she quickly freshened up and decided to take a walk before setting up her appointments. The Hyatt was part of the bustling new Embarcadero Center, adjacent to the financial district, and cable cars stopped at its very door. The ferries and Bay Cruise boats were within a five-minute walk.

Erica made her way through the dazzling lobby out into the mild shining air. As always, she was happy to be in a port city, and this was one of the world's great ones, surrounded on three sides by the ocean. "The Gateway to the Orient"—the phrase popped unbidden into her head, bringing the thought of Steven Kimball in Japan.

She tried to suppress the picture and quickened her pace, walking briskly to the great shopping complex of the Embarcadero Center, where she walked happily for over an hour, taking in the sights and sounds. She noticed several shops that seemed to be potential Erin outlets.

Finally it was time to get to work. Quickly she returned to her suite and set up a series of appointments before having dinner and returning to her room.

It had been a pleasant day, but she felt overcome with jet lag and, after a hasty shower, fell into a deep healing sleep.

Renewed and energetic the next morning, she had appointments through lunch, then took the Golden Gate ferry to Sausalito, passing the deserted gray pile of Alcatraz and, near the ferry-journey's end, the Maritime Museum. Once again she was assailed with treacherous memories, of South Street in New York and the Boston waterfront. But when they landed at the stunning Mediterranean-style community overlooking the blue waters of the bay, in sight of the great Golden Gate, Erica was soon immersed in her work. She decided it would be a perfect location for Erin's Corsair line of beach and nautical clothes.

Back at the hotel that evening she reviewed her schedule. Things had gone so quickly and so well, she decided, that she could leave for Los Angeles the day after tomorrow.

Meanwhile she felt rested and restless, adventurous and daring. Tonight, she resolved, I'll just go out on my own. Why not? She was a free woman, no longer bound by the conventions that used to trouble her. She'd taken the plunge with one man; now she might take it with another. Yet even as she spoke the words silently to herself, she knew they were a lie. No man could ever replace Steven Kimball.

She chose a frankly sensuous dress, street-length but very daring, a chiffon drift of umber bronzes, blues and greens, with a wide, deep V in back that bared her golden, satiny skin. The front V almost reached her waist, but was camouflaged by a wide, soft flounce and offset by long-fitted sleeves.

She wore no ornament but a pair of simple red-gold earrings, and with her sleek hairdo and somber bronze accessories the effect was stunning.

She gave herself one last approving glance in the full-length mirror and took a light pleated raincoat from the closet; there was the slightest misting rain. She was about to leave when the phone buzzed.

"A Mr. Stephen Kimball to see you," the neutral voice said.

For a long moment she was utterly speechless.

"Miss Warren?" the bland voice questioned.

"Yes?"

Still very courteous, but with an edge of puzzled impatience, the voice repeated, "Mr. Kimball is here to see you."

She thought swiftly: I will see him. This time I'll play his game, but even better than he ever played it himself.

"Send him up," she said curtly, adding a belated "please."

With trembling hands she hung up the phone and caught sight of her face in a mirror. Maybe she was fooling herself; maybe she couldn't face the fact that she wanted to see him, wanted it desperately, that she was not playing a game.

But now, in any case, it was too late. The die was cast. Already she heard a tap at the door.

Opening it she was at once overwhelmed by his tall, magnetic presence. He was wearing a faultlessly cut dark-gray suit, a simple white shirt and a wine cravat that contrasted sharply with his pirate's face and thick black hair. His silver eyes were shining.

He held an enormous bunch of red and purple anemones, so large that they almost hid his broad, strong chest.

"Merry Christmas," he said, grinning, and she noticed that for the first time in their acquaintance he seemed a little shy, off balance— totally unlike his usual arrogant self.

He seemed at a loss for further words as he looked her up and down and shook his head. "Oh, Erica," he whispered. "You can't be this beautiful."

Surprised at how calm she sounded, Erica retorted lightly, "Happy new year. Come in." He came in slowly, still studying her with a wary expression. She closed the door.

He was still holding the flowers. Smiling, she took them from his hands and said coolly, "Thank you. These are lovely." Her voice sounded social, placid, and she saw his look of wariness deepen. "Sit down."

She picked up a vase and took it into the bathroom. After filling the vase with water she brought it back into the living room, set it on a table and proceeded to arrange the flowers in a leisurely fashion. He was still standing.

"Do sit down," she urged him in an artificial tone, thinking: I sound like Merry at tea. He obeyed, but she could feel his strange new uneasiness.

Turning from the flowers she looked him in the eye and asked lightly, "How was Tokyo? As exciting as Rome?"

Immediately she could have bitten off her tongue; the reference was obviously to the gossip about him and Arabella. Bad enough that she had even noticed it, much less cared.

A covert glance told her that he had won that round; his strange light eyes gleamed for a second in his dark face and a slight smile twitched at his lips. "Oh, much more," he replied lazily.

"I'm afraid," she said in a cold voice, "that you've caught me at a very bad time. I was just on my way out."

"To meet someone?" he asked soberly and all trace of the smile disappeared. She looked at him, about to lie, but something stopped her. He looked so different, so—lonely.

"No." Again there was that bright glitter in his silvery eyes.

"May I hope you'll join me for dinner?" he asked with real eagerness.

"I'm afraid I've had dinner." He looked downcast again and she added gently, smiling, "But I'll join you for an after-dinner drink."

His face lit up with pleasure and now she felt strange and uneasy, wondering if she was up to playing games.

Very carefully he helped her with her coat and they went into the corridor and entered one of the crystal bubbles. During its descent neither spoke a word, nor did he say anything afterward beyond a terse directive to their taxi driver.

It wasn't until they were seated at a well-placed table in the noted Carnelian Room a few blocks away, gazing out at the stunning view of the city from the fifty-second floor, that he said softly, "I've missed you, Erica. I missed you more than I've ever missed any woman in all my life."

He put out his hand and touched her fingers. She drew her hand away and retorted, "Surely Arabella didn't give you much time for that." She smiled a bright false smile, thinking: This isn't going the way it should. I sound as unsophisticated, as raw as a jealous high school girl. And the touch of his hand, slight as it was, had set off that trembling hotness deep within her.

She looked down at the table, sure that he must have guessed what she was thinking, for he went on in a low urgent voice, "I know that night in Miami meant something to you and *you* know it did."

"But surely not to you," she replied sharply. A waiter was hovering at his elbow.

"We'll order later," Steven said brusquely and the man withdrew at once.

"Shouldn't you be ordering dinner?" Erica asked evasively.

"Don't change the subject, Erica. Besides, I never eat alone," he said jokingly.

"I'm sure you don't," she returned in a sarcastic manner.

His face darkened with a flush. "I didn't mean it that way, damn it. You know, lady, I can't win with you, can I?"

"Not easily." She felt her earlier resolve return, along with a sudden surge of confidence. All he wanted, she thought, was to continúe his little game, to pop into bed while he maneuvered behind her back. "How are things on the Street?"

"You know better than I. I just got back from Japan. I flew here just to see you, Erica, and I've got to go back soon. Go with me."

The suddenness, the effrontery, of his proposal took her breath away.

He grinned at her. "Why not? You like to travel. So do I. And I couldn't find a prettier companion. Besides, your business on the Coast is nearly concluded."

"How do you know that?" she demanded.

"I have my ways, as you know." He smiled at her.

"To my cost," she agreed in an angry voice. "You've had your ways of trying to buy us out."

"You're wrong. You're completely wrong, Erica. Believe me." He looked so serious, sounded so straightforward, that she was appalled at his duplicity.

"How can you look me in the eyes and say that . . . ?" She stopped, fuming, not knowing how to go on.

"I was wrong, too, apparently." His voice was

hard, his light eyes suddenly blank and unreadable. "I thought that something else could move you besides finance . . . besides your grandfather's precious company. But I was totally wrong. Just tell me one thing—if that's all your interest is, what are you doing here with me . . . now?"

"Because I wanted to see just how far this comedy would go," she answered calmly. "You'll go to any length to get what you want, won't you? You've said so often enough before. And the only reason you want me is because I'm the one woman you can't get, Steven."

He stared at her for a long moment and she thought she saw a strange expression flicker in his silvery eyes. Then it passed as swiftly as it had come.

"Shall we go, then?" he asked with stiff courtesy.

"Of course." She kept her voice as cool and even as his.

Silently they left the restaurant. He hailed a taxi and with that same distant gallantry, as if she were a fragile maiden aunt, handed her inside. They sat far apart for the few short blocks to the Hyatt.

"I'll see you to your room," he said neutrally when they had reached the dazzling atrium of singing birds and babbling water.

"That's not necessary," she protested.

"I insist." Again they ascended in uncomfortable silence.

She unlocked the door to her suite. A hard knot

of pain had risen in her throat; she feared that at any moment she would start to cry and she was too proud, too ashamed, to let him see.

But something in her manner attracted his attention. "Erica." His voice was sharp, commanding. "Look at me. Look at me, I said, dammit."

She obeyed, knowing then that the pain and confusion were clear in her transparent eyes.

"Oh, Erica," he said and his voice was suddenly tender. "I'm coming in." He came in behind her and closed the door.

Abruptly he took her in his arms, holding her bruisingly close. His grasp was so viselike that she could not have escaped if she had wanted to. And now she knew that that was the last thing she wanted. He bent his head and his mouth parted over hers.

She felt herself go soft and fluid, flowing against his hardness, answering his wild demand. And suddenly nothing else mattered at all, not Warren's, not his numerous conquests, not his sarcastic, sometimes cruel ways. She could feel his hard hands, the heat and strength of them, through the frail, drifting fabric of her dress and she cried out with longing, raising her hands to his head, pulling him closer.

All too soon she knew the faintness, the dizziness of that familiar longing he had aroused that could not be withstood.

"Oh, Erica, don't fight me anymore," he whispered, his big hands caressing her face.

She could hear the tidelike rush of her pulses

in her ears and lifted her face again for his long caress.

Bewitched and lost, melting against him once again, she did not realize how long the phone had been ringing, or when the ringing had begun.

Chapter Ten

$\mathcal{E}$rica opened her eyes, swaying in his embrace. She drew back a little, asking to be released.

"Don't answer it, darling," he pleaded, trying to pin her to him again with his strong arms, and for an instant she let the summons of the phone go on, hypnotized by his nearness.

But something said to her, Merry. It might be about Merry. "I have to," Erica whispered reluctantly and he loosed his hold.

"Erica?" She was astonished to hear Merry's own voice, crisp and vital over the long-distance wires.

"Merry! Are you all right?"

"*I'm* all right, but I'm not so sure about the office."

Erica prodded, "What do you mean?" She was aware that Steven was behind her, caressing her with his hands in a teasing fashion. With an impatient movement she drew a little away, but he was undiscouraged; he continued his stroking touch with both hands on her narrow waist.

"Hobie Power's resigning as chairman of the board."

"What!" The stately Hobart Power had been known for years to Merry Blaine by that inappropriate nickname. Erica couldn't believe it. He had been a fixture of Warren's for so long that this was almost unimaginable.

"You haven't heard from the attorneys yet?" Merry demanded.

"No. Perhaps I will soon." Erica was uneasy with Steven so near; she wished he would remove his distracting hands.

"My dear, do you realize that Hobie's twelve percent was sold today to Kimco?" Merry said sharply.

Kimco. Erica's skin turned cold. She moved out of Steven's grasp and out of the corner of her eye saw him wander to the other corner of the living room, where he was apparently studying a painting with great interest. Erica was silent so long that Merry repeated her name.

"Yes, I'm here," Erica said, keeping her voice bland and neutral.

"You're not alone," Merry astutely returned.

"That's right," Erica answered brightly.

"Well, my dear," Merry sounded brisk and urgent, "Kimco now owns twenty-four percent of Warren Industries. Something's got to be done, and fast. When are you coming home?"

"Tomorrow," Erica said curtly. "I'll call you as soon as my flight is arranged."

"Very well, my dear. Good night."

Erica hung up the phone and turned to face Steven Kimball. He was smiling at her with a meaningful look from across the long luxurious room; slowly he began to move toward her, holding out his arms.

But when he saw her face he stopped.

"What is it? What's the matter . . . ? Have you had bad news?"

She was so overcome with conflicting feelings that at first she couldn't answer.

"What is it, Erica? Tell me." Steven came to her and tried to take her in his arms again, but she turned away, shaking off his embrace.

"You've got to tell me what it is," he insisted. "Is there something wrong at home? That was your aunt. Is she ill?" He put his hand on her arm.

"Let go of me." Erica spoke coldly through stiff lips.

Mystified, Steven dropped his hand. "What have I done now?" he demanded.

This was the last straw, she reflected hotly. The very day he had, he claimed, flown all the way from Japan just to see her, his financial games were still being played in New York. He's made a fool of me again, she thought savagely, with his damned sexy eyes and mouth, his hands and body.

"I think you know," she answered in the same cold, calm tone. "Why don't you just leave now, Steven?"

"Leave!" His bright silver-gray eyes shone with sudden anger and he grabbed her, staring down into her face. "Not until you tell me what's happened. Not until I know what's going on."

Erica stood passively in his grasp, looking down at the floor.

"I could shake you," he growled, "when you get that stubborn look on your face. Are you going to tell me why you've suddenly turned so cold?" His hard fingers were like steel on her arms.

"Shake me, then." She looked up into his eyes, burning with indignation. "You'll never make me tell you anything. Now get out. Get out of this suite—get out of my life."

He let his hands slide down from her arms to hang at his sides. Wheeling about, she ran into the bedroom and slammed the door. She leaned with her back against it, her feelings in a turmoil.

At last she heard the outer door to the suite slam shut.

He had betrayed her again, that maddening, cold-blooded, lying . . . Erica couldn't think of a name harsh enough to call him.

Struggling between anger and tears she went to the phone and made inquiries about a flight.

* * *

To cheer herself up that dreary January morning, the day of the special meeting of the board, Erica chose a bright-gold wool suit the color of a nectarine; her severe silk shirt was a rich dark brown, striped in turquoise, gold and green. She was thankful for the brightness of the clothes; they seemed to warm her body under her dark coat as she came into the outer office of Warren Industries.

Through the open door of her big corner office she could see out the window to the building snowstorm against a steel-gray sky beyond.

She greeted Jenny warmly, but was puzzled at something in her assistant's manner. Jenny seemed as alert and friendly as ever, but she didn't quite meet Erica's eyes when she put the morning mail on her desk with the agenda for the meeting.

Well, if it's trouble with Paul again . . . Erica was impatient at the idea. Today of all days she needed all the support she could get. The very idea of the coming meeting turned her hands icy-cold and she felt a shaking sensation in her stomach.

Today the board would elect a new chairman. And she realized gloomily that nothing she had done, no matter how big it had seemed to her, could persuade the stuffy members who remained to elect her. Merry's influential preferred block, which could not be used in actual voting but only as a tool of suggestion, had apparently not worked in Erica's favor.

Erica had learned that last night in a long conference with her worried aunt and the attorneys. Kimco's appalling twenty-four percent, added to the others' twenty-seven, still added up to fifty-one, enough to swing the vote in favor of Hobart Power's close friend and natural successor, Marshall Cooper.

The meeting was set for eleven. Until then, Erica kept herself occupied with busywork, trying not to think of what was coming.

But at last it was ten minutes to eleven. She decided to be in the boardroom when the others arrived; the one who was already there, she felt, would be at a psychological advantage. At least duelists had always found it so, she reflected. She shivered. So many sinister ideas were occurring to her.

Jenny stuck her sleek blond head around the door of Erica's office. "Good luck," she said simply and the two words meant more to Erica than she had expected.

"Thanks." She smiled. "Thanks very much."

Erica rose and went into the boardroom, with its long shining table, perfectly aligned chairs and the big glass wall affording a sweeping view of New York harbor. She remembered the last meeting, in October. At least this time George would be absent; that was a great relief.

She was standing by the window, staring out at the harbor and its ships, when Morgan Hunt entered with the favored candidate, Marshall Cooper.

Erica greeted them with bright, false cordiality and rang for one of the women to bring in coffee.

Marshall Cooper returned her greeting with his usual stiff gallantry—the condescending air that always maddened her so. He seemed to imply with every word that a pretty woman like her had no business in a serious place like this. Erica suppressed her annoyance.

Morgan's hello was very cold. "Good morning, Erica," he said flatly.

Erica, for all her anxiety, was amused. He'd gotten over her at last, apparently.

Soon the other members arrived and, with a kind of fussy stateliness, Marshall Cooper, as chairman *pro tem*, pounded the shining table with his gavel and opened the meeting.

The board dispensed first with relatively minor matters on the agenda before moving on to the main issue.

"Now, gentlemen—and Miss Warren," Cooper hastily added with a paternal smile that annoyed her exceedingly, "the next item of business is the election of a new chairman of the board of trustees."

Erica's heart was fluttering in her throat; she took a deep ragged breath and glanced around the table. Her spirits sank at the sight of the hard-faced stuffy men and the cold eyes of Morgan Hunt. Even Morgan would be against her now, she concluded.

She saw Madge Burke, Cooper's grim middle-aged secretary, enter the room and impassively hand a thick folder to Cooper. He thanked her and she withdrew.

Expressionless, Marshall Cooper took ballots out of the folder and asked the member on his left to begin passing them around. "As you know, this election will be conducted by secret ballot. As you all are also aware, a twenty-four percent vote will be by absentee proxy ballot."

He indicated a small stack of sealed envelopes on the table. "These proxy ballots have, of course, already been marked and will not be opened until the conclusion of this assembly's vote."

When Erica received her ballot she turned it over and looked at the two names on it: Marshall Cooper and Erica Warren. In the box by her own name she marked a large firm X, signed and filled in the percentage line. Forty-nine.

Glancing across the table at Morgan, she watched him mark his ballot and turn it face-down on the table. She imagined that there was a spiteful glint in his blue eyes when he returned her glance.

With what seemed to be maddening slowness the ballots were returned to Marshall Cooper. He turned them over and began to read.

"Cooper, ten percent; Cooper, five percent; Cooper, six percent; Cooper, two percent: Cooper, four percent."

That was a total of twenty-seven percent, Erica calculated. Her heart was beating so hard that it threatened to leap into her throat. There was a suspenseful silence around the long table.

"Warren, forty-nine percent." A trace of an ironic smile was on Cooper's thin lips.

I'm the only one who voted for me, Erica thought, humiliated.

But now the mysterious twenty-four percent would cast the deciding vote. She took a sharp breath, feeling the tension among the others. Not, she thought, that there was any doubt.

Cooper opened the sealed envelopes and began to read more quickly. "Warren, two percent; Warren, twelve percent; Warren, five percent; Warren, five percent."

Erica could not believe what she was hearing. The entire Kimco percentage had gone in her favor. The implication was so puzzling, so shocking, that she barely felt the triumph of her victory. Steven Kimball's vote had been for her, Erica Warren.

Why? Because he felt that she would be the perfect puppet during his projected takeover of Warren's . . . an easy managerial mark . . . ? Or was it for an entirely different reason?

She felt the others' bewildered stares upon her; they were confused, no doubt, by the blank look she knew must be on her face as the wheels of her mind whirled swiftly in speculation.

"Congratulations, Madam Chairman." She realized that Marshall Cooper was speaking to her.

"Thank . . ." Her voice was almost a whisper. She cleared her throat and said more clearly, with a calm of which she was proud, "Thank you, Marshall."

Again she glanced at Morgan; his face was

flushed with vexation and he didn't meet her look.

"I wish to make a statement to the board." Cooper spoke again. "I herewith tender my resignation as a member of this board of trustees, which will be presented in writing to the chairman in due course. And I also wish to advise you that I am resigning as vice-president of the Marine Division of Warren Industries."

Erica gasped aloud and her gasp was echoed by Morgan and the other members. Marshall Cooper had been with Warren Industries for more than forty years; only Josh Warren had a longer history with the company. And Erica was dismayed. For all their differences, she had a deep respect for the stodgy Cooper. He was one of the most knowledgeable marine men on the East Coast, if not in the entire country.

"I'm sorry to hear that," she said clearly to him. "The company needs you; your resignation will be a great loss to all of us. I only hope that you may be persuaded to reconsider." She needed Cooper, she realized. And, furthermore, she needed all the rest of the board to remain as a vote of confidence in her leadership. It was a blow to have such a prestigious member resign, especially now.

"I'm afraid not," Cooper said stiffly. "My resignation will be in your hands this afternoon."

"Very well." Erica could see from his steely demeanor that it was useless to argue.

She wanted to say to all of them that she hoped she would justify their confidence in her, but realized in a swift second what an absurdity that would be: None of them had had any confidence in her at all. The only two who had voted for Erica Warren were Erica Warren and—Steven Kimball. It took all her control not to laugh aloud at the grim absurdity of the situation. Her thoughts were still in a whirl over Steven. She realized something else: The fight was not over. It had just begun.

She might lose other valuable men, men she needed to help her build and maintain Josh Warren's empire.

"If there are no further matters to be discussed," Marshall Cooper said, "this meeting stands adjourned."

One of the men snapped off the tape recorder that had recorded the proceedings of the meeting and, awkwardly, the members of the board shook Erica's hand and filed out. There was little conversation among them and she had an uneasy feeling that they had now become her adversaries. How strange it was, this anticlimactic feeling in the face of apparent triumph.

She sat for a moment at the table, looking out at the swirling snow. The wild dance of thickening flakes echoed the scattered confusion in her own mind.

Merry, she thought suddenly. I must let Merry know. At least *she* will join in my triumph.

She hurried into her office and called her aunt.

"I knew it was going to happen."

Erica was astonished at Merry's matter-of-fact acceptance of the news. "*How* did you know?" she demanded.

"I'll tell you later, Madam Chairman," the old lady retorted.

"We'll celebrate tonight." Erica was puzzled at Merry's silence. "Won't we?"

"Unless you have something better to do."

"What's the matter with you?" Erica demanded. She was at a total loss to understand her aunt's bewildering replies.

"Not a thing in the world." Merry chuckled. "I'll be waiting to hear from you." She hung up.

Erica sat back in her chair, trying to puzzle it out. Surely Merry wasn't having an attack of sudden senility; she had never been brighter or more alert.

Jenny poked a tentative head into the office. She grinned. "Congratulations, Madam Chairman." The news had already gotten around, then. Jenny must have heard the others talking. Erica felt a slight pang of guilt; she should have told Jenny at once. They had been through so much together and the girl was the most loyal employee she had ever had.

"I'm sorry you heard it secondhand." Erica grinned at Jenny. "Don't hover there, assistant. Come in and sit down, for heaven's sake. How about lunch with the most unpopular chairman in New York—if not America?" she added wryly.

Jenny came in and took her customary chair. She had a rather peculiar look and Erica wondered what was coming.

"I suppose you've heard about Cooper, too."

Jenny nodded. "Don't tell me you're going to resign as well?" Erica asked with a laugh.

But she was disconcerted when Jenny gave no answering laugh, only smiled tightly.

"What is it?" Erica demanded. "Tell me."

"Well, it's all so . . . awkward. And peculiar." Jenny looked more embarrassed than ever.

"What is?" This wasn't like the usually direct Jenny.

"Paul's job—" Jenny began.

"*Paul's* job!" Erica repeated. "Is he being transferred out of the city—is that it?" she asked anxiously.

"No, oh, no. That's not it. It's the way—it's the one who gave him the job. The man he's working for." Jenny flushed. "He's got a fantastic job with the creative art division of . . . Kimren." Jenny looked at Erica unhappily and turned redder.

"Well, well," Erica commented with forced lightness. "The world's getting smaller and smaller. I can see that it puts you in the middle a bit, though. Because I'm going to be declaring war on your husband's boss. And you know I have plans for you, here at Warren's."

"Yes." Jenny nodded. "And I'm grateful. You know that, too. It's just such a . . . weird situation."

"It is that," Erica said with a carelessness she didn't feel. "But let's not invite trouble; let's wait and see. Shall we? Meanwhile, thanks for letting me know."

Jenny went out, looking more confused than ever.

Suddenly Erica realized that she was weak with hunger; she'd been too nervous to eat breakfast and now it was nearly two o'clock. And Jenny hadn't replied to her invitation to lunch.

She was about to buzz Jenny when the buzzer vibrated under her very finger. "Yes, Jenny?" she responded.

There was an awkward pause, then Jenny said, "Mr. Kimball is here to see you."

Erica's strong curiosity prompted her to answer at once. "Send him in."

She snatched a small mirror out of her drawer to check her face. It was all right. Then she wondered why it was so all-fired important to look nice for him. All she wanted was information; whether or not she charmed him was irrelevant.

At the same time she had a feeling that she was lying to herself. She had never been able to resist him. Not until now, she thought grimly. She was never going to run away from him again—just face him squarely and fight it out.

The door opened slowly and he came in with a tentative, solemn air. He was wearing a dark-gray, extremely conservative suit with a shirt of dazzling whiteness, but his tie was a brilliant crimson; it drew the eye irresistibly, and she saw that it was patterned with tiny pirates.

How appropriate, she thought. "Good afternoon," she said calmly, staring at him coolly. His thick black hair was cut shorter, but it still sprang up from his brow with vitality and wildness. He looked back at her, though his expression was unreadable.

"I hope I'm not disturbing you," he said formally.

"Not at all," she answered with equal formality. "Won't you sit down?"

With a still-blank face he said, "I don't have much time, I'm afraid. I have to get back to Japan and my plane leaves Kennedy at four. I wanted to leave these. That's all." She saw then that he was holding two fat manila envelopes. He put them on her desk.

"Good-bye," he said. "And good luck." With one last look at her he turned on his heel and left the office.

She wanted to cry out to him to wait, wanted to ask why he had voted for her. A hundred questions buzzed in her brain.

But it was too late. He was gone.

Erica leaned back in her chair, feeling a sharp sense of loss, an emotion that truly surprised her. She had been feeling so belligerent when he walked in, but now . . . She wondered if she would ever see him again. There had been something so final about his good-bye.

With trembling fingers she opened the first envelope. On top was a long handwritten letter. Under the letter were stock transfers from Kimco to Erica Warren. In the other there was a document attesting to the creation of Warren's Kimren Division, to be headed by Erica Warren Kimball.

Erica Warren Kimball. He had meant to change her name to Kimball. What had happened? She stared at the strange exciting name, remembering with dismay how cold she had been to him in San Francisco; he must have been planning this then.

The letter—the explanation must be in the letter. Eagerly she withdrew the letter from the first envelope and began to read.

My dearest Erica,

I've been in love with you ever since I first saw your picture in a paper, a picture of the Baby Tycoon, somebody just like me. And yet so different, with those big brown eyes, like a doe. A lady with guts and brains, imagination.

She read the sentences again, overcome with shame and tenderness. Then, eagerly, she scanned the following paragraphs.

Ever since that afternoon when I pulled you out of the harbor I've been afraid of you. That's quite a joke, isn't it? Kimball, the Takeover King, afraid of a little thing no higher than his chin, a hundred and ten pounds wringing wet—which you assuredly were that first afternoon. I was afraid to ask you to marry me. After all, I thought, why should you need me? You've always had everything—beauty and power, money of your own. I figured you didn't need me or any man. I was flip and rude, to hide my fear.

But I couldn't get you out of my mind. And I decided maybe I could make you need me—if not by making love to you, at least by getting so tangled up in your life that you'd have to see me just to get me out of your hair.

Erica's heart was beating like a triphammer. The letter explained so much, so much. It made so many things clear.

It went on:

That night, with Arabella at the theater, I was only doing a favor for a friend. And then, in Rome, she began to show up everywhere I went. It was damned awkward, but she was always around when some blasted photographer showed up, making it look as if we were, as the columnists so nastily put it, "an item." I knew you had seen some of that nonsense when you asked me about Rome in San Francisco.

There was never anything between us. But she was useful, I must admit. I found out from her when she was in her cups that George Blaine and Morgan Hunt were out to get you—Hunt through marriage, George through Hunt and other slimy operations of his own. I decided to keep an eye on Warren and buy up as much stock as I could get my hands on, then turn it over to you. As you will see from the transfers, I have done so.

I should have told you something about all this, I know now, and not let you think that it was just a simple takeover plot. But old habits die hard; I've always liked the cloak-and-dagger side of finance. And I wanted to get rid of the deadwood around you, which I know very well how to do, being an old hand at this game. I knew that if I offered them enough, plus some favors which only I could come through with, I'd have them. And I did.

The loan came from me; I'm the largest stockholder in that bank. I thought you should have your chance and I didn't want you going anywhere else, for personal reasons.

Erica grinned and read on eagerly.

As you guessed, it was no coincidence that I turned up in Boston, Miami and Houston. Then you had to leave and the best I could do was that gangster-funeral display of flowers. I guess I just lost my head, as the kids say. Mrs. Blaine loved it, though. She's great, by the way.

The letter looked blurred and Erica felt a hot moisture under her lids. She blinked it away and continued.

Miami was the greatest thing that ever happened to me in my life. I hoped against hope that after that we'd get married. So when you ran off it knocked me off-kilter. As you know, I still didn't give up. But I've given up now. After San Francisco I can see there's no chance for me with you.
I'll have the Kimren Division changed to the name of your choice and the papers made out to Erica Warren as soon as I get in touch with my attorneys. Aside from that I guess there's nothing much else to say. Except that I will always love you and I wish you the best of everything.

Steven

"Oh, Steven," Erica said aloud. "I've been such a fool."

Steven Kimball was the only man who had ever shown her what love was like, the only man she'd ever be able to love as long as she lived. And now he was gone. Now he was lost to her.

Unless . . . She glanced at her watch. Twenty-five till three. She could hardly believe that so much had happened in so little time. Her whole life had changed in the space of half an hour.

Four o'clock, he'd said. His plane left Kennedy Airport at four. She'd never make it, never. But she'd have to.

Quickly she dialed the airport and tracked down his flight. Was the plane, she queried desperately, on time?

"There may be a slight delay," the indifferent voice told her, "because of the weather."

Without even a thanks Erica slammed down the phone and ran to the closet. She threw her coat on, picked up her purse and ran through the outer office past an astonished Jenny.

Every delay was maddening. The elevator had never seemed so slow, the Mercedes so reluctant to start. At last she was speeding toward the airport. The roads were getting very slippery from the storm and she prayed that she wouldn't have an accident.

Twice she was forced to stop at the scene of other accidents and afterward drove a little more cautiously. But as she neared the airport she sped up again.

With a screech of brakes she pulled up in the parking area and began to make her way to the impossibly distant terminal. She had forgotten to put on her hat and snow settled on her hair and stuck to her lashes. She could hardly see; she blinked the snow away and hurried on.

She felt her breath grow short; it was hard to breathe in the driving snow, going at that pace on her fragile high-heeled shoes. They were soaked now, but she didn't care. She had to get there before he was gone.

At last she reached the terminal and waited impatiently for those ahead of her to go slowly through the revolving door.

Freezing and soaked, teeth chattering, she hurried through the main waiting room and headed for the international lounge. Glancing at her watch she saw that it was already five minutes to four; it was hardly believable that her trip had taken so long.

She looked up at the board. The Tokyo flight was now listed as on time.

Erica hurried to the boarding area. "You can't go in there, miss," a guard warned. "They've already boarded."

"I've got to get to someone on the plane. It's a matter of life and death!" she cried out.

The man hesitated, examining her disheveled appearance.

"Please!" she begged. "You must page someone on the loudspeaker. Steven Kimball."

The guard lifted his brows at the name. "I'll try, miss," he said kindly. "But I'm afraid it's too late."

Desperately she waited behind the barrier. The guard hurried to a hidden room and then, to her relief, she heard the loudspeaker booming Steven Kimball's name.

She peered through the smudged glass, her heart in her mouth. The sign had been wrong, she concluded, thank heaven.

The doors of the plane were still open. But now the driving snow obscured her view; another departing plane moved between her and the one she was so desperately watching.

It seemed an age before she saw a tall dark man with snow on his hair striding toward her from a long way away. He was still too far away to recognize. Oh, no, she thought, what if it isn't him? What if he decided not to answer?

Her tear-dimmed snow-blinded eyes peered along the distant walkway. The man came nearer. It was him; it was Steven, she realized with exultation.

No one else walked like that, carried himself like that—like a buccaneer who owned everything around him.

Her heart was drumming so hard that she was afraid it might leap right out of her body and her arms and legs were trembling. She had never fainted in her life, but she had an awful feeling that she might faint now.

As he came nearer and nearer she was frightened by the look on his face; he was unsmiling and the brightness of his silver-gray eyes revealed nothing. She wondered whether he had even seen her or recognized her.

He hadn't, she was sure, and her heart sank.

Two tall men had moved ahead of her, blocking her from Steven's vision as they waited to board another flight.

Now she felt too faint and frightened to wave or call attention to herself. What if he hadn't really meant that last part of the letter—that he would always love her? What if he had already resigned himself to a life without her?

She saw him speaking to the guard, who

turned in her direction, pointing; yet it was obvious he still couldn't see her because of the two tall men.

But then she saw Steven striding toward her. He had seen her now and there was a wide incredulous smile on his face; his white teeth were dazzling against his tanned skin, his eyes bright and piercing, looking directly at her.

She hurried forward to the barrier and he grabbed her in his arms, his briefcase falling to the concrete.

"Oh, Erica," he said against her hair. "I was a damned fool to leave."

"I'm the one who's been a fool. You did all that for me and when I think of the way I rewarded you—"

"Never mind," he said, smiling. "A fool couldn't have built Erin. . . . A fool wouldn't be handed Kimren."

Then, as if they were alone in the world, he bent his head and kissed her. Her head was spinning; she relaxed against him, returning his kiss with abandoned fervor, no longer caring who saw them.

Around them people began good-naturedly to applaud.

Erica grinned. "For someone who tries to keep a low profile you're not doing so hot," she said.

"You're all wet, as usual," he teased her. "Like old times."

"I'm afraid you've missed your plane."

"Tokyo will have to wait." He stooped, picked up his briefcase and put his arm tightly around her. "First we've got to change your name. And I think you should let your aunt know. She's waiting."

Erica laughed. So that was what Merry had been talking about.

She moved closer to him as they walked back to the terminal. Even through their heavy clothes she could feel the power and heat of his hand on her body and she looked up again into his remarkable eyes, dazzling, unforgettable, the color of her love's first silver fire.

Silhouette Desire
15-Day Trial Offer

A new romance series
that explores
contemporary relationships
in exciting detail

Six Silhouette Desire romances, free for 15 days!
We'll send you six new Silhouette Desire romances
to look over for 15 days, absolutely free! If you decide
not to keep the books, return them and owe nothing.

Six books a month, free home delivery. If you like
Silhouette Desire romances as much as we think you
will, keep them and return your payment with the
invoice. Then we will send you six new books every
month to preview, just as soon as they are published.
You pay only for the books you decide to keep, and
you never pay postage and handling.

------ **MAIL TODAY** ------

Silhouette Desire, Dept. SDSE 7K
120 Brighton Road, Clifton, NJ 07012

Please send me 6 Silhouette Desire romances to keep for
15 days, absolutely free. I understand I am not obligated
to join the Silhouette Desire Book Club unless I decide
to keep them.

Name_____

Address_____

City_____

State_____ Zip_____

This offer expires June 30, 1983

MORE ROMANCE FOR
A SPECIAL WAY TO RELAX

$1.95 each

1 ☐ TERMS OF SURRENDER Dailey	22 ☐ ALL THAT GLITTERS Howard
2 ☐ INTIMATE STRANGERS Hastings	23 ☐ LOVE'S GOLDEN SHADOW Charles
3 ☐ MEXICAN RHAPSODY Dixon	24 ☐ GAMBLE OF DESIRE Dixon
4 ☐ VALAQUEZ BRIDE Vitek	25 ☐ TEARS AND RED ROSES Hardy
5 ☐ PARADISE POSTPONED Converse	26 ☐ A FLIGHT OF SWALLOWS Scott
6 ☐ SEARCH FOR A NEW DAWN Douglass	27 ☐ A MAN WITH DOUBTS Wisdom
7 ☐ SILVER MIST Stanford	28 ☐ THE FLAMING TREE Ripy
8 ☐ KEYS TO DANIEL'S HOUSE Halston	29 ☐ YEARNING OF ANGELS Bergen
9 ☐ ALL OUR TOMORROWS Baxter	30 ☐ BRIDE IN BARBADOS Stephens
10 ☐ TEXAS ROSE Thiels	31 ☐ TEARS OF YESTERDAY Baxter
11 ☐ LOVE IS SURRENDER Thornton	32 ☐ A TIME TO LOVE Douglass
12 ☐ NEVER GIVE YOUR HEART Sinclair	33 ☐ HEATHER'S SONG Palmer
13 ☐ BITTER VICTORY Beckman	34 ☐ MIXED BLESSING Sinclair
14 ☐ EYE OF THE HURRICANE Keene	35 ☐ STORMY CHALLENGE James
15 ☐ DANGEROUS MAGIC James	36 ☐ FOXFIRE LIGHT Dailey
16 ☐ MAYAN MOON Carr	37 ☐ MAGNOLIA MOON Stanford
17 ☐ SO MANY TOMORROWS John	38 ☐ WEB OF PASSION John
18 ☐ A WOMAN'S PLACE Hamilton	39 ☐ AUTUMN HARVEST Milan
19 ☐ DECEMBER'S WINE Shaw	40 ☐ HEARTSTORM Converse
20 ☐ NORTHERN LIGHTS Musgrave	41 ☐ COLLISION COURSE Halston
21 ☐ ROUGH DIAMOND Hastings	42 ☐ PROUD VINTAGE Drummond

MORE ROMANCE FOR
A SPECIAL WAY TO RELAX

43 ☐ ALL SHE EVER WANTED Shaw

44 ☐ SUMMER MAGIC Eden

45 ☐ LOVE'S TENDER TRIAL Charles

46 ☐ AN INDEPENDENT WIFE Howard

47 ☐ PRIDE'S POSSESSION Stephens

48 ☐ LOVE HAS ITS REASONS Ferrell

49 ☐ A MATTER OF TIME Hastings

50 ☐ FINDERS KEEPERS Browning

51 ☐ STORMY AFFAIR Trent

52 ☐ DESIGNED FOR LOVE Sinclair

53 ☐ GODDESS OF THE MOON Thomas

54 ☐ THORNE'S WAY Hohl

55 ☐ SUN LOVER Stanford

56 ☐ SILVER FIRE Wallace

57 ☐ PRIDE'S RECKONING Thornton

58 ☐ KNIGHTLY LOVE Douglass

59 ☐ THE HEART'S VICTORY Roberts

60 ☐ ONCE AND FOREVER Thorne

LOOK FOR *AFTER THE RAIN*
BY LINDA SHAW AVAILABLE IN JANUARY
AND *SEASON OF SEDUCTION* BY ABRA TAYLOR
IN FEBRUARY.

SILHOUETTE SPECIAL EDITION, Department SE/2
1230 Avenue of the Americas
New York, NY 10020

Please send me the books I have checked above. I am enclosing $_____
(please add 50¢ to cover postage and handling. NYS and NYC residents
please add appropriate sales tax). Send check or money order—no cash or
C.O.D.'s please. Allow six weeks for delivery.

NAME _____

ADDRESS _____

CITY _____ STATE/ZIP _____

Silhouette Special Edition

Coming Next Month

Tender Deception by Patti Beckman

After the crash, memory gone and appearance altered, Lilly Parker began to search for her identity and found Kirk, her husband . . . who had fallen in love with the woman she'd become!

Deep Waters by Laurey Bright

Dallas fought her attraction for anthropologist, Nick, from the steaming jungles of Engima Island to the moon-silvered beaches . . . but where he was concerned she knew she would be easily conquered.

Love With A Perfect Stranger by Pamela Wallace

One night aboard the Orient Express they met— and carried away by romance, Torey gave her heart. Now, trip over, Peter West would leave her life forever . . . or would he?

Mist Of Blossoms by Jane Converse

Singing star Brett Wells was tired of being chased by women. So how could Carolyn tell him of her love when he insisted that they remain just friends?

Handful Of Sky by Tory Cates

Shallie had to make her way in rodeo, a man's world, and Hunt McIver's help was invaluable. But the man himself remained a mystery . . . one she longed to solve.

A Sporting Affair by Jennifer Mikels

Alaine's heart never had so much as a sporting chance of escaping unscathed once she met ballplayer Doug Morrow, the charismatic pitcher who made it clear he would have things his own way.

15-Day Free Trial Offer
6 Silhouette Romances

6 Silhouette Romances, free for 15 days! We'll send you 6 new Silhouette Romances to keep for 15 days, absolutely free! If you decide not to keep them, send them back to us. You pay nothing.

Free Home Delivery. But if you enjoy them as much as we think you will, keep them by paying the invoice enclosed with your free trial shipment. We'll pay all shipping and handling charges. You get the convenience of Home Delivery and we pay the postage and handling charge each month.

Don't miss a copy. The Silhouette Book Club is the way to make sure you'll be able to receive every new romance we publish before they're sold out. There is no minimum number of books to buy and you can cancel at any time.

This offer expires June 30, 1983

Silhouette Book Club, Dept. SRSE 7B
120 Brighton Road, Clifton, NJ 07012

Please send me 6 Silhouette Romances to keep for 15 days, absolutely free. I understand I am not obligated to join the Silhouette Book Club unless I decide to keep them.

NAME_____

ADDRESS_____

CITY_____ STATE_____ ZIP_____

READERS' COMMENTS ON SILHOUETTE SPECIAL EDITIONS:

"I just finished reading the first six Silhouette Special Edition Books and I had to take the opportunity to write you and tell you how much I enjoyed them. I enjoyed all the authors in this series. Best wishes on your Silhouette Special Editions line and many thanks."

—B.H.*, Jackson, OH

"The Special Editions are really special and I enjoyed them very much! I am looking forward to next month's books."

—R.M.W.*, Melbourne, FL

"I've just finished reading four of your first six Special Editions and I enjoyed them very much. I like the more sensual detail and longer stories. I will look forward each month to your new Special Editions."

—L.S.*, Visalia, CA

"Silhouette Special Editions are — 1.) Superb! 2.) Great! 3.) Delicious! 4.) Fantastic! . . . Did I leave anything out? These are books that an adult woman can read . . . I love them!"

—H.C.*, Monterey Park, CA

* names available on request